MW01125140

SALVATION IN CHAOS

CKMC1
LINNY LAWLESS

CHAOS KINGS
MOTORCYCLE CLUB

*To Cathy —
Linny Lawless*

Copyright October 2018 by Linda Lawson
All rights reserved.
This book is a work of fiction. Some of the places
named in the book are actual places found in Virginia.
The names, characters, brands and incidents are either
the product of my imagination and used fictitiously.
Any resemblance to actual persons, living or dead,
events or establishments is solely coincidental.
This book contains mature content and is intended
for adults 18+ only.

Cover Model: Darren Birks, Book Covers and More
with Darren Birks Photography
Cover Design: Cosmic Letterz Cover Design
Editor: Teri Hicks
PA Services: Mikki Thomas

To Norman. My Biker Man, Best Friend and
Husband

CHAPTER ONE

RACHET

I took a long swig of beer to chase down the third whiskey shot I just shared with my club brother, Gunner. We rode three miles from Stayford County, Virginia to the Eastern Maryland Coastline for the twentieth annual Bike Week event. The other members of our club, Chaos Kings MC, rode in a group earlier that day. Gunner and I needed a quick stop in at a biker bar called Buckhorns Saloon, one of the many bars that opened for the long weekend to host thousands of bikers for the annual event. Raindrops splattered on our gas tanks as we parked the bikes in the lot and planted our kickstands down.

I sat with Gunner at the bar and scoped out the scene around me. Most bikers were already getting their heavy induced buzzes going, fueled by alcohol and other illegal substances. A red-haired woman with huge paid-for tits rode a mechanical bull next to the stage, as southern rock cover band played the song "Mustang Sally". The red head moved her hips back and forth to the rhythm of the slow bucking bull while horny bikers hollered and whistled. She pulled her sparkly tank top off and swung it around a few times before throwing it to the crowd.

The redhead reminded me a little of Mandi back home. She was a sweet butt I'd been bangin' for a few months. Fuckin' her was fun and she was a wildcat, likin' it on the rough side. And that was fine with me cause I only knew good, hard poundin', rough fuckin'. And that's all I was gonna get out of it. But I needed a break from her sometimes. Small doses of Wildcat Mandi were enough. The long ride with Gunner to Bike Week was the right prescription for what I needed.

It was the same crazy biker shit, just a new year. You drank a lot, listen to some live music, get your dick sucked, or get laid.

I kept my head down and lifted my eyes up to survey the place. I scanned the other side of the horseshoe-shaped bar. A biker waited to be served by one of the bikini wearing bartender girls; two women cackled and talked amongst each other; some were whooping and hollering, wiggling on the barstools to the live music. But the cute petite brunette with some really sexy pouty lips caught my eye. She was sitting by herself, wide-eyed, staring at her beer and peeling the label off the wet bottle with her finger.

I nudged Gunner, "Twelve o'clock, brother. See her? Brunette, nice lips. Nice dick suckin' lips?"

He looked in that direction and saw her, "Yeah… She's fuckable."

Just when I started to imagine those pretty lips wrapped around my hard dick, a bald, middle-aged biker in a jean vest rubbed up against the girl's back. He leaned in from behind her and whispered something in her ear. She didn't seem to know the guy and didn't look as if she liked it either. I tilted my bottle up to my mouth and downed the rest of it.

"I'm goin' for it. Try and get my dick wet… I'll be back."

I left the barstool next to Gunner, walked around the bar and stood behind the bald biker. I tapped him on the shoulder. The moment he turned to me, I grabbed the front of his jean vest, "Hey fuck-wad, this one belongs to me. So, get your whiskey dick *off* my property and walk!" I growled, baring my teeth.

I released his jacket and he raised his hands up, "Ok, ok, Man. My bad. I'm walkin'."

But before I even turned back to the girl, she grabbed a back-pack and jumped off the barstool. She was quick and moved through the sea of drunk bikers, blue jeans and black leather, toward the parking lot outside.

So, she likes to be chased… And caught, I said to myself and followed her path outside.

CHAPTER TWO

SAM

I bumped into a woman, making her spill her drink down front of her shirt. "Hey! Watch it, Bitch!" She yelled, but I was already five steps away. Once I was out in the parking lot, heavy raindrops landed on my face.

I didn't know where to go, or what to do next, but I knew not to go back in there. I had to keep a low profile. Not be noticed. Not be seen. Then that perverted biker rubbed up against me and whispered in my ear where on my body he wanted to rub his dick on. The moment the tall biker intervened was my opportunity to make a break for it.

The lot was full of at least a hundred motorcycles parked under lit up street lamps. There was a dark gravel path that led to the main road toward the ocean's coastal highway. I wrapped my arms around myself and started to walk in that direction, as the rain fell, soaking through my hair and clothes.

"You're not gonna get away that fast!" Big hands captured my arms and spun me back around. I looked up and up, at the tall biker who just called me his property.

He released me and tilted his head, "You scampered off like a scared little bunny rabbit! And you didn't look like you were enjoying that dipshit rubbing his whiskey dick on you either." His voice was low and deep.

My mouth was suddenly dry and I didn't know what to say to the hulk size biker. It was dark, but I could make out that his dark hair was a bit long, past the collar of his cut and a bit messy too. I imagined his beard covering a chiseled square jaw. I could make out tattoos that covered both huge muscled arms with intricate designs.

I mustered up the use of my voice, "I had to get out of there. I. I... can't go back in there!" I hoped he didn't take my stuttering as an opening to try and finish what the other biker tried to start with me.

"Well, you're not gonna walk out here alone. Not in the dark and not in this rain."

"But I can't go back in there! I can't —"

"Ok. You don't have to do anything you don't wanna... I see you got your own lid there on your pack. Get on my bike and I'll take you where you wanna go."

I stared at him for a moment. So far, he didn't try anything with me when he could have, or say anything to set me off to run again. He was so much bigger than me, but he seemed safe. I followed two paces behind him, back to the parking lot full of bikes. When he stopped, I didn't and my face smashed into his broad back. He turned around when I stepped back and chuckled low, "I don't just let *any* chick on my bike without even knowing her name... They call me Ratchet."

"I'm Sam... And thank you for getting that biker to leave me alone."

The side of his mouth lifted in a smirk. He was probably amused at what he was looking at - a soaking wet mess. "Not a problem. Now let's ride and get you somewhere dry."

When I got on his bike, I kept my hands to myself. I leaned back, away from Ratchet.

"Hold on, Little Rabbit. Don't want you scampering off again."

He was thick as a tree and smelled of whiskey, cigarettes, leather and rain. I placed my hands on the sides of his waist. He kicked the stand up with his booted heel, twisted on the throttle in first gear and rode us out of the parking lot onto the main road.

Ratchet road me twenty blocks up the coastal highway. I didn't have anywhere to stay or go for that matter. He must have figured that out when he pulled us up to a stoplight.

He turned his head toward me, "I have a motel room three blocks up. You wanna go there and dry off? Don't worry. I won't rub up on you, Little Rabbit."

"Ok," I squeaked out against his ear.

He had a room at one of the many beach motels along the coastal highway with a queen-size bed. The dresser and nightstands looked about thirty years old, beachy photos with seashells and seagulls hung from sandy colored walls.

Ratchet handed me a dry towel, I wiped my face and dried my hair with it. I looked down at myself. My nipples were hard as little rocks, as they pressed up against my light blue tank top. I slid the towel down to cover myself. He suddenly looked away as I looked back at him. He took his leather cut off and hung it on the back of a wooden chair. I recognized his club patch – The Chaos Kings MC – a grinning skull, wearing a Viking helmet, on top of two crossed battle axes.

"Do you know any Chaos?" He asked me as I looked at his colors.

"No… but I know of your club…"

Reaching into the side pocket, he pulled out his

cigarettes and a flask. He twisted the top open and took a sip of whatever was in it. He offered it to me. "Take a sip. It'll warm you up some."

I took a small sip and coughed a few times from the burning taste. It felt warm sliding down my throat, my chest flushed from cold to warm. I handed the flask back to him and he set it on the nightstand.

Ratchet took a few steps toward me. I leaned my head back to look up at him. He was well over six feet tall. His messy dark hair was soaked and hung down over his brow. He was so close I could see that his eyes were a pale shade of brown with little tiny specs of amber in the irises. My stomach did a summersault and I felt my neck and cheeks flush again with warmth, but not from the whiskey.

He stared down at my mouth as I opened it, not knowing what to say with him so close to me. It was different than sitting behind him on his bike. He reached up and lightly grazed his calloused thumb across my lower lip. "I want to taste those lips of yours, Little Rabbit…"

He leaned in and covered my lips with his. His tongue slid into my mouth slowly at first. He tasted so good that my tongue couldn't help but swirl around his. I suddenly moaned into his mouth and his huge hands grasped my hips. He squeezed just a little, moving even closer to me.

I felt him hard against my fluttering stomach. He released me from the slow kiss. "I'm not going to stop, Sam. Unless you want me to," he grumbled low, his eyes staring so intense with the hunger I had seen in the eyes of other men. Other men who hurt me. Violated me…

I stepped away from him and my fight or flight mode suddenly kicked in. "Please stop!" I pleaded, "I mean… sorry… just please don't hurt me… I'll do whatever you want."

He released me and stepped back, "Shhhh… It's ok, Little Rabbit. I'm not gonna hurt you…"

He watched me for a few moments then turned and walked over to his duffle bag. He pulled out a dry t-shirt and handed it to me. "I'm gonna go take a piss. You can get out of those wet clothes and wear that t-shirt. It'll be too big on you, but at least it's dry."

CHAPTER THREE

RACHET

I went to the bathroom and took a piss with a semi-hard on. I didn't intend on frightening Sam. But I couldn't resist getting just one kiss from her. I didn't expect my dick to get hard that quick from just a kiss either. When I came out of the bathroom, Sam was in bed under the covers wearing my t-shirt. She laid on her side, her back to me. *She probably needed sleep*, I thought. It was clear to me the little rabbit was running away from something or someone and was trying to blend in with the crowd at the Buckhorns Saloon. She didn't want to attract any attention it seemed. That's why she shot out of there so fast.

I went to the nightstand, grabbed the flask and smokes and headed out the door. I leaned up against the wall next to motel room window and took a drink from the flask. I lit a smoke, taking a long drag and watched it drift away as I exhaled. I stood there and kept watch. Was Sam a sweet-butt from a club? She wasn't wearing any properties, just that tank top, where I could see her perky hard nipples poking through. My dick jumped again.

The Chaos Kings didn't treat their women like sheep. They could wear properties signifying they belonged to a club member, but it was a show of respect and high regard. Women were never beaten or used in any way for money, or drugs or anything else for illegal gain. If a woman was mistreated by a member, the Chaos Kings gave him a good beat down and the piece of shit was kicked out of the club.

My head felt fuzzy when I flicked away my smoke, but I had only taken a few swigs from the flask. I went back into the room. Sam was still asleep, curled up in a ball on her side under the blankets. Then the room started to spin and I felt so fuckin' sleepy. I stripped off my wet clothes and slid under the covers next to Sam's small frame. Laying a forearm over my eyes, I was out like a fuckin' light.

* * *

I opened my eyes against the throbbing pain pounding in my head. I let out a groan, sitting up and swinging my legs off the bed. "Fuck….me…," I grumbled, rubbing my temples.

Sam must have slipped something into my flask the night before, because I felt the effects of a drug-induced hangover. I opened one eye and looked down to see my wallet lying next to my wet jeans on the floor. Snatching it up, I opened it. Only a one-hundred-dollar bill was there, the other five were gone. I turned toward the side of the bed Sam slept on and saw my t-shirt bunched up in the same spot where Sam had slept. She was gone.

I shook my head, "Son… of… a … Bitch... The little rabbit got away. And with some of my fuckin' cash."

* * *

The rest of Bike Week was just a blur. Thousands of bikers swarmed the local bars along the Maryland coastline. The parking lots were jam-packed with motorcycles. It was like spring break for bikers, where all the debauchery, burnouts, loud pipes, live music, alcohol, drugs and women wearing next to nothing congregated once a year. I searched for Sam at every place I stopped in at with my brothers. I surveyed every bar, every crowd, but never found the sly little rabbit.

"So that pint-sized chick pulled a fast one on ya, huh? Stole your money too... It's not fuckin' easy to slip something over you, brother," Gunner said as I scoped out Shark Fins, one the bars we frequented that week.

I didn't respond and the questions kept churning in my fuckin' head. Did she belong to an MC? Was she someone's property? Would I ever see her again? I didn't care about the stolen cash. I only knew her name and that she was on the run. But when I did *find* her, I was going to get those questions answered. I couldn't get her out of my mind. I should have just fucked her, but I stopped kissing her sweet lips when she got frightened. I couldn't blame her for running off since I *did* tell her I wouldn't try to rub up on her that night.

* * *

A week later

I noticed three Harleys parked outside the Crow Bar as I pulled in ahead of Gunner and shut the ignition off on my Night Train. They belonged to the Hell Hounds MC.

"See what I see?" I said to Gunner nodding toward the bikes. He turned the ignition off his Road King after he pulled up alongside me. "This might not be a happy endin' to a good day's ride."

Gunner shrugged his shoulders, kicking his

stand down, "Yeah… Well, hopefully they're payin' their bar tab right about now and fuckin' leavin'."

The Hell Hounds were a diamond club, a one percenter club, an outlaw club. They wore a three-piece patch with their top rocker, Hell Hounds, their center patch depicting a black dog with three snarling heads and a bottom rocker "Virginia". Their chapter resided in the same county as the Chaos Kings. They made their money in dealing meth and prostitution. Every member had a criminal record, from drugs, prostitution, robbery, to assault, rape and even charges of murder, but no convictions. The Steel Cage, a strip club across the county line, was their main hang out. There were rumors about suspicious illegal shit conducted behind closed doors at the club. Sometimes I even heard about ties to the Russian Mafia. Some of my brothers had frequented the club before. Not me. I didn't want to have to end violent shit that the Hounds would start, especially wearing my colors in a club they claimed was their turf.

Today was the perfect day to ride out west to the Shenandoah Mountains. Just me and Gunner. Now I had to keep my good mood in check, hoping that nothing ugly would happen inside with the Hounds.

Greaser, the owner of the fine establishment, popped the tops off a couple of beers as we grabbed some stools at the bar. I took the first long guzzle of nice cold brew and lit a smoke. "How's it hangin', Grease?"

"It's hangin', Ratchet. How was Bike Week? I see you and Gunner came back in one piece," Greaser replied, his graying hair greased up fifties style in a pompadour.

The Crow Bar was the typical biker bar, dimly lit by Tiffany lamps hanging low and two pool tables in the back along with a digital jukebox. The song "Crazy Bitch" by Buckcherry was playing at that moment. I took in the scene and found the Hounds through the cloud of cigarette smoke coming from the pool tables. Two Hounds were playing a game of pool. The third Hound sat in a chair, medium build, dark hair. And Sam was sitting on his lap, looking right me.

CHAPTER FOUR

SAM

I knew it was Ratchet the minute he walked in. He was so tall and wide, taking broad steps as he walked with a confident swagger. Not cocky, just assured. He grabbed a bar stool, lit his cigarette and tilted the beer bottle up to his lips. Then he turned in my direction and his eyes locked on me. Sitting on Sid's lap.

Please don't say anything... just look the other way, I said to myself, both hoping and dreading that I would ever see Ratchet again. I thought every day about that rainy night at Bike Week when he kissed me. And I kissed him back. He tasted of whiskey and cigarettes. That weird feeling of butterflies fluttered in my stomach when I felt his hardness pressed up against me. Then something snapped. The warm and tingly feeling suddenly frightened me. Images flashed through my mind. Hands were grabbing and bruising my flesh. Teeth biting, fists punching, my body violated, repeatedly.

I was stunned but relieved that Ratchet stopped. Even when I could see the hunger in his eyes, he stopped. No man had ever stopped before. That's why I felt guilty for slipping a good dose of crushed up Xanax into his flask when he was in the bathroom. I pretended to be asleep while he was outside drinking from the flask. When he passed out next to me, I took his t-shirt off and put my wet clothes back on. I pulled his wallet from the pocket of his jeans, snatched up five hundred dollars and shoved it in my pocket. Put my boots back on, grabbed my back-pack and slipped out of the motel room unnoticed by anyone.

Sudden pain shot through the back of my scalp as a handful of my hair was snatched violently and pulled, flinging my head back. "What you lookin' at, Bitch?" Sid whispered next to my cheek with a clenched jaw.

His fist still in my hair, his eyes turned toward the bar, where Ratchet and his brother were sitting. "Well... Well... Is that the Chaos you fucked that night at Bike Week? That night you fuckin' took off and left me?"

"I didn't fuck him, Sid...," I stammered, "I just took his money..."

"Yea. Well, at least you had enough fuckin' smarts to get the cash after you got done suckin' his cock."

Sid was the Vice President of the Hell Hounds MC. He was sadistic and liked to hurt me in any way he could without killing me. I was pretty much his property. He could do things to me and no one would stop him. He used me in every conceivable way, whether to help push drugs or pass me around for even more money.

He had a medium build and he was quick. His dark hair was always spiked out and messy. His dark eyes had a sinister gleam to them. He didn't have a club name. His real name was Sid, some called him Sadistic Sid.

He pushed me off him and stood. I staggered ahead a few steps to stop my fall. He grabbed my arm, "Come on. Let's go. I guess I have to show you again why it's not good to run from me ever again bitch... Rusty! Tweek! Put the fuckin' sticks down. Let's go play out back."

Sid pushed me forward to walk ahead of him down the hall toward the bathrooms and out the back door. Once outside, I turned around to face him. He stepped up to me, looked into my eyes and smirked. His eyes slowly roamed down my body. "Rusty, take her arms and keep her still."

Rusty was suddenly behind me. He took both my arms and pulled them behind me. I had to arch my back as Rusty brushed his reddish greasy beard against my cheek. He inhaled deep and moaned into my ear as he exhaled, "Mmm... you even *smell* like a whore..."

The switchblade was out of Sid's pocket and my tank top made a ripping sound as he sliced it down the middle with the blade. He flicked the blade in between my bra and it snapped open. I felt the night air on my breasts, making my nipples harden against my will.

"You have gorgeous fuckin' tits, Sam," he pressed the tip of the blade against my right nipple, "If you ever run from me again, I will cut your tits off. Then what will you be? A worthless cunt without tits."

How many times had I been threatened? Beaten? Humiliated? Raped? My fight or flight mode kicked in. And this time my fight mode was leading the race, matching the speed of my fast beating heart.

"Go ahead, Sid. Do it," I heard my own voice. And Sid heard it too.

"*Bitch*!" He yelled.

The last thing I remembered was the back of his hand contacting the right side of my face. Then everything went black.

CHAPTER FIVE

RACHET

When I saw the little rabbit sitting on that Hell Hound's lap, I knew *who* and *what* she was running from. I nudged Gunner to look my way, "Hey, brother. There's the girl who stole my money at Bike Week."

I didn't wait to hear Gunner because I was off my barstool and heading toward the piece of shit Hound with a fistful of Sam's hair. He pushed her little body off his lap and propelled her down the hall toward the back door. The other Hounds were right behind them.

"Hold up, Ratchet. I'm comin' with you."

I heard Gunner tell Grease to get us both another beer. He was two steps behind me.

CHAPTER SIX

SAM

I *was drowning. I could see the surface of the water and tried to come up for air. But hands held my arms and legs under, just beneath the surface, pulling me down deeper. I needed to break that surface for my next breath of air to keep me alive. I started to scream underwater, bubbles escaped from my mouth and floated upward past me to the surface.*

"No!" I heard my own cry and opened my eyes. I was in a bed. My head on a pillow. I smelled leather and looked down. I was covered in a big heavy black leather jacket. I looked back up and into the eyes of the Chaos King, sitting in a wooden chair a few feet away. The same man I drugged and stole money from.

I was suddenly up and sitting on the edge of the bed. Ratchet reached me in a heartbeat, "Its ok, Rabbit. You're safe." He came to sit next to me.

"What happened?" I asked as I looked around. It was a small bedroom with a full-size bed, a nightstand and a wooden chair. The walls were white and empty of any pictures or décor.

"I found you knocked out cold behind the Crow Bar. Those Hell Hounds roughed you up a bit." His brows were drawn together. "I borrowed Greaser's truck and brought you here to my clubhouse."

The dream of drowning. Fear and anxiety jolted through me. "I gotta go. Sid and the Hounds are looking for me now."

His big arm came around me, preventing my attempt to get off the bed. "Hold on now. You might have a concussion. You should get checked out first."

I felt the heat from his body, his big arm wrapped around my shoulders. "I'm ok. Really. I can't stay here. I have to go."

"I'm gonna talk to my Prez and VP. We'll figure somethin' out. You can stay here in the clubhouse for a few days."

I leaned away from him, placing my hands on his hard chest. "No... Thanks, Ratchet, if I stay here at your clubhouse, Sid and the Hell Hounds will just find me again. I don't want you and your club to become part of all this."

He pushed off the bed and walked toward the door. He stopped and ran his hand through his messy dark hair. He shook his head and turned back around. "I know now why you were runnin', Sam. And you *are* still runnin'. If you want out, I'll help. My club will help. This is my tribe, Sam. The Chaos Kings. We're good people. We take care of our own. You're safe here. I can protect you."

It didn't register what this hulk of biker said to me. Safe? Protected? I was never safe. No one ever protected me. And why would he want to? He could have done anything he wanted to me that night in his motel room. Just like Sid and all those other men.

"We'll get you situated with some clothes and things first." His eyes roamed my body, but he couldn't see much with the huge black leather jacket that covered it. "What size do you wear, Rabbit? You weighed next to nothing when I carried you to the truck... I can ask one of the ol' ladies to do some shoppin' and get you some clean clothes."

CHAPTER SEVEN

RACHET

She could have gotten killed. Maybe if I didn't look in her direction at the Crow Bar, that fucker wouldn't have knocked her out cold and left her there in a rain puddle out back. My fault I put her in that jam. Well, it was done. The Hell Hounds just left her there. My heart pounded hard against my chest when I found her. I cradled her head in my lap as I drove her to the clubhouse, hoping she'd come to. I wasn't going to let her scamper off again. And not back to the Hounds.

I called Rocky, my Prez. Asked him to meet me at the clubhouse. I got some coffee with lots of cream and sugar for Sam. She sat in the bedroom I put her in the night before and headed out to the parking lot, lighting up a smoke. I greeted Rocky and our VP, Spider when they pulled into the lot on their bikes.

Rocky was as bulked up as me, keeping his head bald and sported a beard that was more grey than it was brown. Spider was leaner in build, a bit tall and lanky with long dark hair that he usually kept tied back. The chicks loved to braid it for him and he never turned down an offer.

"Prez... VP...." We gave each other a round of brotherly hugs.

"How's it hangin', Ratchet?" Rocky released me from his bear hug.

"Gotta situation and need to bounce some things off you both."

They knew about that night at Bike Week and how Sam laced my flask and took off with my cash. I rehashed what happened last night at the Crow Bar and that Sam was under my protection now. I needed my brothers to back me up. That was going to help her get out.

"Well, brother... We don't mingle with those fuckin' dogs. They're bad news. Been bad news for a long time. They leave us alone. We leave them alone. Sounds like this girl's in deep with them. Maybe she just needs a break. You could just bang her. Have a little fun and when she's had her fun, she might want to go back. What's it about her that's got you wantin' to help her? Maybe she doesn't want help."

"I got Mandi to bang. And she's already a fuckin' handful."

"I bet she is, brother!" Rocky landed a playful jab on my shoulder.

"Yeah, yeah. And I don't need another handful. Sam's been banged up bad before. I'm sure of it. And I bet worse than how I found her last night."

"Ok, Ratchet. Let's give her a few weeks. She can stay here at the clubhouse for a bit till you can figure out what her game plan is. We'll be here, brother. Anything you need. Hell, we could use some help to keep this clubhouse from turnin' into a shitty dive bar after a weekend of partyin' and fuckin'!"

"Hells yeah, Ratchet. I'm with Rocky. Do what needs to get done to help the girl out," Spider reaffirmed what Prez said.

Helping around the clubhouse was a solution to how Sam could pay me back the money she stole. And it was a way I could keep an eye on her.

The next day the right side of Sam's temple was a bit red and would probably turn a shade of purple before it would heal completely. I gave a wad of cash to the Prez's ol' lady, Madge and she went to the local mall and bought some clothes for Sam. The look on her face when she opened the bags full of girl stuff was like a kid at Christmas who didn't expect anything. And then there it was – that amazing smile.

A smile that made my dick jump and made the front of my jeans suddenly tight. I needed to stop picturing her lips around it or stop wondering what her pussy tasted like. Felt like. And I had a sure bet she tasted sweet and felt so fuckin' good as I buried my dick deep inside her.

Then my thoughts sobered up. I had another sure bet that she experienced fuckin' hell with the Hounds that she wouldn't want to share with me. I remember the hell I was living in when I was a kid. That hell was James Racette the First. I was James Racette the Second. Named after my father. What he did to me. What he did to my mother.... Telling me I was just like him.

And that's why I had to keep those thoughts of Sam out of my head and focus on helping her. She needed her space. Not to be crowded, especially from another man who only thinks about fuckin' her every minute of the day.

She seemed to be on the petite side naturally, but I knew she needed to get a little more food in her to fill out that sexy curvy figure she had. I told her to get dressed in some of the clothes Madge picked out for her because I wanted to take her out for breakfast. It would be good just to have some alone time between us and talk.

I was standing by my bike, finishing up a smoke

and waiting for Sam. She walked out of the clubhouse toward me and my heart skipped a few beats. She used one of the showers in the clubhouse and wore some of those new clothes – a flowy red tank top and some tight ass jeans that hugged her in all the right places, along with her black riding boots.

"Madge got the right sizes for me." She looked down at her new clothes. So, did I.

"Huh? Oh… yeah. She did good, Sam." I had to peel my eyes away from her for a moment and coughed.

A light breeze carried the scent of her still damp hair to my nose. She smelled like strawberries or something fuckin' fruity. There went my cock again. The sweet scent and those tight ass jeans made my cock jump yet again… She looked back up at me with that smile.

"You look really nice, Sam…," I grumbled, sounding like a fuckin' dork.

It was a pleasant ride to the diner with the little rabbit sitting behind me on my bike. The trees were budding and things were blooming again. I hoped the spring air helped Sam's mood. I knew she had experience riding on the back of a bike and I could sense her relaxed posture behind me. She didn't have to, but she wrapped her arms around my waist and her inner thighs were pressed up against mine.

I pulled the bike into the small parking lot at the Knotty Pine. It was a breakfast diner that had been in business since the nineteen fifties in the old town of Front Royal. Breakfast diner in the front. Biker bar in the back. We went to the front and sat in a booth. We both ordered a full plate of eggs, sausage, hash browns and toast. I didn't know how she did it, but she finished her plate the same time I did. She leaned back against the booth and burped. It was the cutest thing.

"Oops. excuse me…," Sam giggled. And that was fuckin' adorable too.

I couldn't help but smirk. "We need to get this out of the way… About my money you took at Bike Week."

Her smile faded, "Yeah I know. I want to apologize for that. That was wrong of me."

"And you spiked my flask, Sam. What did you put in it?"

"Xanax… a few doses…"

"Well that was the right number of doses. I'll accept your apology, but you're not gettin' off that easy. I talked to my Prez and VP. You can pay me back by helpin' at the clubhouse for a few weeks. Help keep get the place cleaned up. This weekend is Memorial Day and the Rolling Thunder ride to the Wall. It's also a weekend-long excuse to party at the clubhouse. It's open house to other bikers who are friends of the club. You can help the other girls behind the bar. That will make us even. Deal?"

"Yes. It's a deal, Ratchet."

"It's James. My name is James Racette. Club calls me Ratchet."

I didn't know why I told her my real name when I only knew her for a few weeks. And I'm not sure why her eyes lit up when I told her.

"It's a deal, James."

We pulled into the clubhouse lot and there she was headed right to us. Mandi... I forgot to fuckin' call her the night I brought Sam to the clubhouse. Mandi. Tall, blond with long legs that fit just right wrapped around me when I pounded into her. She had nice tits too, but they were paid for and didn't have that natural sexy bounce to them when I watched her ride my dick. Mandi liked it rough too, though. She liked the faint bruises I left on her hips and ass because of my rough grip. Sometimes I didn't realize how hard my grip was. But instead of complaining, she begged for more. She was a sweet butt and fucked some of the other club members. But for now, I was her club flavor of the month.

"Who the fuck is this short skank, Ratchet?" She yelled across the lot as I kicked the stand down.

Sam got off, her eyes locked on Mandi as she approached us.

"She's not a skank, Mandi. Her name's Sam and she's helpin' out around the clubhouse for a few weeks. Sam this is Mandi."

"Yeah, I'm sure she's gonna help around the clubhouse," Mandi turned to Sam, "By giving out blowjobs behind the fuckin' bar!"

"Just cool down, Mandi. I'll meet you inside. We'll talk."

"Fuck you, Ratchet!" She barked at me and flipped Sam off with a smile and walked away from us to her white Nissan. She spun tires and gravel, leaving the lot.

Not only was I going to watch over Sam, but I would also need her to steer clear of Mandi. I knew I was going to have to fuck her fierce just to reassure her that everything was fine and normal in her fucked up shallow world.

Sam turned back to me, "I don't want to cause any problems between you two."

"Sorry about that. She sees you on my bike, so her claws came out. Just stay clear of her for now, Sam."

CHAPTER EIGHT

SAM

Riding with Ratchet that morning helped me get some fresh air into my lungs and clear my fuzzy head. The wind was pushing against my face and the scent of things blooming felt good. I smelled his leather jacket and his male scent which both comforted me and made me dizzy with this yearning I had between my legs. I never felt this before being so close to a man. He was so big and tall which frightened me like that rainy night in his room. But he didn't try anything on me or make me feel uncomfortable. I was not used to that either.

It's not a surprise to me that he had an attractive girlfriend, someone as handsome and kind as him. I was only used to other women who belonged to the Hell Hounds and some were just as hateful and vicious as the Hell Hounds. I stayed clear of them as much as I could.

Bikers from up and down the east coast were coming into town for the Memorial Day holiday ride in the Rolling Thunder event to the Vietnam Memorial Wall in Washington DC. I was never able to enjoy or have any fun with Sid and the Hell Hounds. Only tense situations and confrontations with other bikers, fights in the back alleys of bars, harassing other women if they got bored with me.

It was Saturday night and I was looking forward to helping at the clubhouse. Not only were members of the Chaos Kings coming out to celebrate, but their biker friends from up and down the east coast would be there. I think I made a good impression on the President's lady, Madge and some of the ol' ladies and friends of the club this week.

The Chaos Kings clubhouse was much nicer than the Hell Hounds. From what Ratchet, well James, told me, the huge warehouse was on a lease. The President, VP and other club members put their money together to pay the monthly rent and the property owner was good with the club constructing it the way they wanted. It was all legit. There was a bar that was very elaborate for what I was used to and the other half was a wide-open area with old couches, huge floor rugs, two pool tables, some dart boards and even a digital music jukebox. The members all were gifted with skills, from carpenters, mechanics, electricians, HVAC and even a few tattoo artists. They even sectioned off the other side of the bar and built walls for a few private bedrooms with bathrooms and showers, for anyone who needed a place to crash and recoup from a crazy weekend.

I helped as much as I could with cleaning the rooms, bathrooms and the bar area. Ratchet introduced me to some of the ol' ladies and women that came by to hang out after work or help with things around the clubhouse.

I met Tanya, a long-time childhood friend with some club members. She was very kind to me and had such a care-free personality, like a butterfly fluttering around to talk to everyone. They all seemed to like her. She had light brown hair and very pretty with eyes that always seemed to be smiling, even if she wasn't.

"We're gonna have a fun time this weekend. I guarantee it, Sam. I'll introduce you to some of the other gals here. We call ourselves the Chaos Coven … muwahaaa haaaa…" Tanya's laugh was low.

"Some of us can be little witches and bitches sometimes, but not all of us are back-stabbers… Oh and watch your back with Mandi. She's got her claws in Ratchet right now. I don't know what Ratchet was thinking. Well, sometimes they think with their other brain I guess."

I smiled at her last comment. Men do have two brains.

"Well, it's true, Sam. Men think ninety percent of the time with their dicks and the other ten percent of the time with their other brain."

"I met Mandi the other day. She hates me already since she saw me on Ratchet's bike. I'll just steer clear of her."

I met Madge, the President's ol' lady. Parts of her body displayed some beautiful ink. Some were old school and some were more colorful and detailed. She wore red lipstick that emphasized her red hair and fair skin and her style of dress was rockabilly pin. I thanked her for picking out the nice clothes for me.

"Anytime, Hon. You're cute as a button," Mag said hugging me.

"I must have done a fantastic job because Ratchet can't take his eyes off you," she tilted her head, winking.

I didn't agree with her on that. I was plain Jane. I didn't have any women friends I could relate to, or do fun girl things like going clothes shopping together or girls night out.

Ratchet came by the clubhouse during the week and brought me breakfast and lunch during breaks. He worked with his brother, Gunner at Mack's Towing Company. He'd have a smoke then head back to work. I didn't say much to him. I didn't know *what* to say. He didn't ask me any questions or pry, which made it easier for me. And his eyes. That chestnut color. They mesmerized me, drew me in, making my stomach do somersaults. Sometimes I caught him staring at me. Like he was struggling to ask me or tell me something, but never did.

But I kept my wall up. Stayed alert. Fight or flight. Each morning I woke up with a nagging feeling. Would this be the day Sid comes to take me back with him and the Hell Hounds? Did he know I was hiding out here with the Chaos Kings? Would he hurt Ratchet? Would he kill him? Would he kill me?

That's why I didn't tell Ratchet anything. Where I came from. How I became Sid's property. My life with Sid and the club. The horrible things they made me do. I was afraid that he would see me as just another used up club whore. He had his Chaos brothers and a girlfriend. Why did even want to help someone like me?

CHAPTER NINE

RACHET

It was Saturday night and the clubhouse was packed. Cigarette, cigar and that sweet scent of weed surrounded me. All my brothers were here. So were a large number of friends of the MC ready to do damage that some would regret by the end of the holiday weekend.

I had a few shots of cheap whiskey with Gunner, along with four or five beers already, surveying the crowd and watching Sam's every step as she helped behind the bar. She wore a black tank top with a pink skull on it and another pair of those tight ass jeans hugging her plumper curves that I helped with. I made sure she had three meals every day which helped put a little bit more weight on her. And it showed. My dick still got hard every time she smiled, or when I watched her little sweet ass as she walked around the clubhouse.

"So, looks like Sam is gettin' along ok at the clubhouse, brother. She did a damn good job of cleanin' up around here. Made it look like a party clubhouse rather than the typical shithole," Gunner just said what I was thinking. Other than watching Sam's every move, I noticed how the place looked better and smelled better too.

"Ever get your dick wet? That *was* your plan that night at Bike Week, right?" He chuckled.

"No, brother. Not gonna fuck her. She's been through some bad shit. I don't even know much about her. She won't talk about it. I'm just makin' sure she gets some food in her. And she is helpin' around the clubhouse as payback for takin' my money. Besides, I have Mandi to get my dick wet. She's all about how good she looks, but she likes a good bangin' anytime I want it."

Gunner crashed his bottle to mine, "Nothin' wrong with that, brother."

A few more shots of whiskey and a couple of smokes later, I had a good buzz goin'. The jukebox was playing "Crazy Bitch" by Buckcherry and some of the chicks were dancing on the pool tables, gyrating their hips and shakin' their asses. Some tops started comin' off too and my club brothers and their friends were cheering the chicks on. Not only was this a 'damage your liver weekend' it was also 'who's gonna get laid and how many times weekend'.

Even with the loud music, hollering and cussing, I still had my sights on Sam. I watched her every move. And every motherfucker there checked her out at least once. She was popping the top off a bottle and handing it to one of my brothers everyone calls Magnet. As in – 'Chick Magnet'. He never had a problem finding a chick to bang. He was a sweet talker and the chicks said he was good lookin' and good at fuckin' too. Whatever Gunner just said didn't register when I saw Sam smile at Magnet. That same smile she gave me, making me hard in my jeans and my heart pound at double speed in my fuckin' chest.

My legs moved. I sauntered over to her, tossing my empty bottle in a trash barrel. I was behind the bar and directly behind Sam. I placed both my hands on the bar, caging her in between them.

"Don't spend any more time on this one, Magnet. She's with me."

Hearing my voice, Sam snapped her head around her eyes level to my chest. And I got a quick whiff of her hair. That sweet scent of strawberries again…

"That's cool, Ratchet. The night's still young," he smiled and winked at Sam and left his bar stool to find another chick to sweet talk.

I was super curious and looked down at her as he walked away. "So, what did Magnet say that made you give him that smile Sam?" The whiskey shots were doing the job and spiking my dominance over her.

"He just told me it was nice to see a fresh face behind the bar. So, I thanked him and smiled. That's all."

"Well I didn't like it, Sam…"

"I just smiled…"

"I didn't like it…," I repeated.

Her lips parted and I couldn't stop staring at them. So soft, I wanted to taste them again. I reached up and grazed my calloused thumb across her bottom lip. And her eyes suddenly had a spark to them.

"When I saw you sitting there alone at the bar the first time, do you know what was in my head, Little Rabbit?"

She shook head, but kept her eyes locked on mine.

"I pictured these sexy lips of yours wrapped around my hard dick."

She gasped and her eyes widened. And that's when I leaned down and licked her lower lip.

"But now that I've tasted your lips, I wanna taste your pussy. And I bet it tastes as fuckin' sweet as this mouth of yours."

My eyes moved past her lips to the curve of her tits. Her nipples were hard, like little pebbles pressed against her tank top. "And I bet you wanna know what my tongue would feel like in that sweet little pussy don't you, Sam?"

My dick was rock hard and pressing up against the front of my jeans. I was standing so close to her and I knew she could feel it against her like she did that night in the motel room. I reached up and traced my finger around the hard nipple over her tank top lightly. Making little circles and felt it bead up even more.

"I can see you're not wearing a bra, Little Rabbit," I mumbled low so that only she could hear.

"Heads up, Ratchet. Two o'clock… Mandi…" Gunner broke my concentration on her delicious tits.

I looked out over the crowd and saw the wildcat coming straight my way.

"Best I stop, Sam… I'll let you get back to it." I stepped back from her. Her hard nipples still poking through her tank top.

CHAPTER TEN

SAM

When James stepped away from me, I was breathing funny and felt a tingling between my thighs. My nipples were hard and they ached. When he touched one, it sent a jolt of liquid warmth from my nipples down to my pussy. I had never felt these things before. I noticed his hard-on against me too. He was gentle and his touch didn't repulse me, like Sid's or other men who hurt me before.

As he walked away, I inhaled a deep breath to

gather myself. I turned back to the bar and helped hand out bottle after bottle of beer to club members and bikers. And I hoped that Mandi didn't see what just happened between us. I looked their way and she was pointing her finger at his chest and saying something, her eyes wide. She looked right at me and I looked away.

Ratchet seized her forearm and pivoted her around smacking her rear and directing her to walk in front of him toward the bedrooms past the bar. She swayed her hips, her jaw jutted out, in her cut off jean shorts that showed off her long legs and red stiletto heeled sandals.

I leaned on the bar folding my arms in front of me. I watched everyone having a good time, gathering myself, trying to calm my racing heart. Gunner appeared and sat on the barstool.

Some of the men of the Chaos Kings, like Ratchet and Gunner, were ruggedly handsome. Gunner was also covered in tats like most of them, with dark brown hair. He always wore a five o'clock shadow on his square jaw. He had blue eyes that had an appealing squint to them like he'd been in the sun most of his life.

"Hey Sam, any more Buds back there?" I dug through the ice in one of the tubs, twisted the top off and handed it to him.

He took a gulp and grinned. "Thanks, darlin'. You've been a major help around here this week. Just wanted you to know that in case Ratchet didn't," he said with a wink. Glad Ratchet didn't see that.

"It was the least I could do... And thank you...for last week."

"Not a problem. You were knocked out cold. Glad it was us that found you back there." Gunner turned around to watch some of the girls dancing on the pool tables. "Nice," He chuckled, nodding his head as the girls bump and grind on each other.

"Chaos Kings are good people, Sam. Ratchet is good people. I don't know much about you, but you don't have to be afraid of us. We're not like the Hell Hounds. We don't beat on women."

"I can see that, Gunner. Not something I'm used to though."

"Yeah... well... the world is a big place. And it's fucked up sometimes. There are good people. Bad people. And there's scum lowlife's like the Hell Hounds. You're in a better place here than there, Sam."

He took another swig from his beer. "Just have a good time tonight. We Chaos definitely know how to do that!" he winked again and sauntered over to a group of his brothers and other bikers.

CHAPTER ELEVEN

RACHET

I followed Mandi into the bedroom next to the one Sam was sleeping in for the past week. She turned around as I shut the door and latched onto me in two blinks. Clutching my Cut with both hands, she planted a hard kiss, then drove her tongue into my mouth. She had that cinnamon taste from too many shots of Fireball. I nudged her off me and broke that sloppy kiss.

"Oh, Ratchet. Why do you wanna rub up on that skank? I heard she belongs to the Hell Hounds

MC. And you know those dogs fucked her way too much. She's all used up," she whined looking up at me, batting her fake glued-on lashes.

At that moment, I *really* looked at Mandi. And I saw the *real* her. I realized there was nothing attractive or sexy about her. The fake tits, fake lashes, fake smile, fake howling when I fucked her. She liked it. But I didn't. Sam was real. The real smile, real tits that would look so good bouncing as she rode my hard dick. I couldn't get those images of her out of my head.

"I'm only telling you once, Mandi. Leave her alone. She's been through shit. Shit you could never come through and survive. She doesn't belong to the Hounds anymore. That's why she's here. You know my history. I wasn't gonna just leave her at the Crow Bar."

"Baby, I do know your history. Your dad... your mom. That wasn't your fault what your mom did. She took the easy way out. She wasn't woman enough to handle men like you. Like your dad. Strong men... So alpha-"

I seized her arms. "Not woman enough, huh? My piece of shit father was not an alpha! He was a fuckin' bully. A sadistic fuck and a waste of space." I pushed her off me.

"Fuck off, Mandi. Go find another cock to suck. I'm done with the fake."

She was on her knees. Unbuckling my belt, looking up at me, "Oh please, Daddy... I'll suck your

cock off really good… You can choke me with it…
please, Daddy."

I bent and pulled her up off her knees, "No,
Mandi. I'm done. "

I released her, turned and walked out the
bedroom door. And that was the end of fake. I
wanted real. Sam was real.

* * *

Two AM. I was exhausted. There were drunk and
stoned bodies passed out in the rooms, on the
couches and the pool tables. Ratchet stayed clear of
me for the rest of the night. He walked out of the
bedroom without Mandi. He avoided looking at me,
frowning and clenching his hands into fists while
walking out of the clubhouse to a lot full of parked
bikes. Mandi came out a few minutes later. She
walked past the bar and glared at me. She blew me a
kiss and winked. She veered and sauntered over to of
a group of bikers. Her chest arched a bit, showing
cleavage and she started to dance to the music on the
jukebox. She gained the attention she was aiming for
and took a drink of one of their beers.

I searched for Ratchet, over the passed-out
bodies and my heart sank when I couldn't find him.
I wanted to be next to him. He must have left the
party after he stormed out of the room where he left
Mandi.

I was the last one left awake, so I dragged my

feet down the hall to the room that I had slept in for the past week. I opened the door and I jumped. Ratchet was there sitting on the bed and resting up against the headboard. His black riding boots were crossed at the ankles, smoking a cigarette while looking right at me.

The side of his mouth lifted into a half smile. "Didn't mean to scare you... Just didn't feel like going home tonight. Figured I'd stay the night here with you. Come on over. I won't bite." He looked down at his hand patting the empty space next to him.

My heart skipped a beat hearing his low rumbly voice. He blew out a drag of smoke, still waiting for me to move.

"I don't think Mandi would like that idea."

"Don't worry about Mandi. I'm done with her. It's over between us... There was really nothing there in the first place. Just realized it tonight like a fuckin' match was lit."

I still didn't move.

"You can't just stand there all night, rabbit. I'm not getting off this bed."

"Promise you won't crowd me again as you did earlier tonight?"

"Well, if you're gonna stay in the clubhouse, then you better just get used to it," he raised his voice a bit louder than I'd heard before.

I was too tired and let him win the argument. I walked over and sat in the empty space next to him.

He grinned then looked off at the wall in front of him, taking another drag off the cigarette.

"Get some sleep, Sam. It's been a long night." I laid down on my side, away from him. Closed my eyes and was fast asleep.

Ratchet was sleeping, his arm draped over me, snoring lightly in my ear. I slowly slipped out from under his arm, went into the bathroom, brushed my teeth and hair and went out to the bar to make some coffee. I brought back two hot cups to the room and he was the same way as when I left – asleep and snoring. I walked up to the edge of the bed and watched him. There was no tension in his face. Then his one eye opened.

"I hope all the snoring didn't make you scamper off, Little Rabbit," he said with a sleepy grumble.

I couldn't help but smile. "No... I just thought you would like some coffee when you wake up."

He stretched and sat up against the headboard and rubbed his eyes with the palms of his hands.

I handed him a cup. "I wasn't sure how you like it. I put both sugar and cream."

He took a sip and smiled, "That's exactly how I like it, thanks..."

I still didn't understand why he smiled and looked at me that way because once he knew all the things I had done I wouldn't see that smile again...

"Now, come back here."

I sat next to him taking a sip of my coffee.

"How did you get mixed up with the Hell Hounds?'

His question was the one I dreaded. I avoided looking at him and stared at my cup. I didn't even know where to begin or what I should tell him.

"I have been Sid's property for a long time," I said quietly, staring down at my cup, "I left him and the club that night you found me at Buckhorns. I snuck away and tried to blend in with the crowd..."

"Well, you are one brave woman I know that."

"Sorry about the money. I didn't have any and I was afraid Sid and the Hounds would find me with you. So, I took off. I didn't know you. And I didn't want you to get involved."

"But he did find you..."

"Yes... I didn't know where to go that night and just started walking down the coastal highway. When they found me, I showed Sid the cash and told him I partied with a few Chaos Kings."

"And that's why I saw you with them at the Crow Bar?"

"Yes. And he saw you and Gunner too. He was still angry and I was still paying for what I'd done by running away."

"So, he took you out back and hurt you. I found you with your top and bra ripped open... "

"He's done worse."

His jaw ticked and he stared off again.

"So, you lived in hell? I know, Sam.... I lived in hell too, a long time ago..."

His brown eyes turned soft when he turned to look back at me. He leaned in and kissed me. It was not heated. But it still made my stomach flutter. It was soft; gentle. And it felt nice.

CHAPTER TWELVE

RACHET

*T*he door is shut and I'm sitting on my bed. But I can hear him yelling at my mom.

I hear a crash. Sounds like one of the plates of dinner she made for us tonight smashing against a wall and clattering in pieces to the floor.

"God damn mother fuckin' BURDEN you are. You AND that scrawny ass kid cryin' and pissin' his pants in that bedroom!" My father's voice was deep and sounded like thunder.

I hear my mom whimpering.

"What good are you?"

Father must have lost his job, again. Making it seem like it was mother's fault. My fault…

I woke up. Sam's back nestled up against my chest. My arm wrapped around her. She was breathing steady. Sound asleep. I slowly turned over trying to stay quiet hoping not to wake her; slipping on my jeans and flannel shirt. I didn't bother buttoning it up and slid my boots on before grabbing my smokes and heading outside to check on the bike.

The sun was starting to rise. I lit a smoke and raked a hand through my bed head. I felt that nagging pain in the back of my throat again. That nagging pain that started so long ago… I could never get back to sleep when those memories invaded my dreams.

How could I protect Sam if I couldn't even protect my own mother? Sam had been through fuckin' hell with those Hounds. She was so physically small; I was amazed she was even still alive. She was brave… She had the courage and the will to do what she needed to do to stay alive. I couldn't picture someone like Mandi push through that kind of shit.

I took another drag off my smoke, deep in thought, when I felt that familiar soft rub against my shin and then against my calf. I looked down. There it was. That cat. It started to come around about a month ago. One night, I was shit-faced taking shots of whiskey with Gunner and Wez. I was *never* going to admit it to the brothers, but I needed a minute to get some air or I was gonna hurl my lunch right in front of them. I remembered staggering over here. I rubbed my eyes until I saw stars behind my lids and felt that soft rub like the one currently against my shin. It just looked up at me and made that purring sound that I figured cats made. I never had any pets growing up. I didn't know much about cats or dogs but I liked them.

The cat must have been a stray and found its way to the trash dumpsters out back. It had a dull grey color with some black stripes. It looked like it had been living and fending for itself for a while. Its fur was matted everywhere and smelled like it rolled around in grease spots from the lot. I stared at it for a few minutes while it kept walking back and forth, rubbing its greasy fur on my lower leg. I blinked a few times and warned it to stop moving, or I was gonna blow chunks.

It was back. This time I was sober, so I got a better look at it.

It looked thin and would probably eat something.

"Stay put."

I headed back into the clubhouse to the pantry. There was always a variety of canned food stashed there.

Cats seemed to like fish in the cartoons I watched when I was a kid, so I grabbed the small can of tuna, opened it with a hand twist can opener and headed back outside. The cat was in the same spot where I left him, walking around in circles, making that purr noise. I knelt and set the can in front of it. It didn't take the cat more than five seconds from looking at it, to smelling it and then chowing down.

"Take it easy, bro. It's all yours."

I headed back in, wanting to check on Sam, but I needed to rub one out first. I was hard as a rock when I stepped into the shower. I lathered my cock with soap, making it slippery. Gripping and stroking it, I pictured Sam. The image of her sweet tits arching up to me, her nipples as hard as beads, her pussy slick and wet. I gripped my cock tighter and stroked it fast. I started to use both hands, pumping it fast and hard. My head fell back, my heart racing, my breathing shaky. I suddenly exploded. My cum shot quick, hitting the tile wall.

I brewed some coffee for Sam this time, remembering how she had done the same for me. She sat up on the bed, yawned and blinked her eyes a few times and then they locked on me. She had the cutest bed head I had ever seen on a chick. I leaned down, handing her a cup.

"Didn't want to wake you earlier. You were sleeping good."

She took a sip, closed her eyes and moaned.

"Thank you. I did sleep good."

I sat down on the bed. She began to talk. To tell me things and I listened.

CHAPTER THIRTEEN

RACHET

I t's Monday morning and I'm at the shop with Gunner, starting our weekly shift towing service calls.

"She's lived with the Hounds a long time brother," I told Gunner while I drove one of the flatbed tow trucks.

"Well, she's not now," he replied.

"And I'm keepin' it that way."

"She's done a hell of a job around the clubhouse. She's a little on the quiet side, but I can understand that."

Gunner looked over at me and smirked, "I can tell you have a soft spot for her, Ratchet. What do you call her? Little Rabbit?"

"Yeah. That's because she scampered away like a rabbit at Buckhorns that night at Bike Week."

Gunner lived in the basement at my house. He was like a brother from another mother. He sponsored me when I was probate for the Chaos Kings. I rode for years and knew a lot of local clubs, some legit, and some diamond clubs. I was a hang-around a little while first before Gunner approached me. He served two tours in Iraq, came back a war veteran and we just clicked.

"I'm gonna talk to Sam about movin' her into my place. I know Chaos is not at all like those filthy fuckin' Hounds, but just get her to my place, help her get grounded and on her feet."

"Good idea, brother. A girl like that deserves a fresh start," he agreed and my mind was set.

CHAPTER FOURTEEN

SAM

A sunny and chilly morning and Ratchet wanted me to ride with him, Gunner, Wez to the mountains. We started out early morning. The temperature rose as the sun got higher spreading its warmth on the budding trees and all things growing green for the summer. As I held on to Ratchet, I closed my eyes and smelled the fresh morning air and listened to the roar of the pipes. The vibration was felt from my ass, down to my thighs. Ratchet's huge warm palm and fingers wrapped around the bottom of my left thigh. That liquid warmth and fluttering in my stomach started up again inside me. He squeezed just a little. I squeezed him back with both thighs against his hips.

We rode into the small town of Front Royal. The town had a long history dating back to the late 1700's. Naturally situated in and surrounded by the Shenandoah Mountains many called it 'Hell Town' where rugged men lived and worked and were less than law-abiding. They drank and got into brawls.

We pulled into the tiny parking lot of the Knotty Pine, the diner and bar Ratchet took me for breakfast. The four of us took a seat at one of the booths inside. Ratchet slid into the booth right next to me; so close that our thighs touched. He raised his arm over and laid it on the back of the booth behind me. He turned to me and winked, His brown eyes were so warm and kind, with a hint of heated want.

Gunner and Wez slid into the booth across from us. I knew Gunner some, but this was the first time I met their other Chaos brother, Wez. His real name was Devon, but his club called him Wez from the villain in the movie 'Road Warrior'. He wore his hair in a mohawk cut. Both arms were full sleeves of tattoos, including some detailed designs on his neck. Not surprising as he was an ink artist himself and did all the work on the Prez's ol' lady, Madge.

"Wez, show Sam that thing you do," Ratchet said, with a nod to me.

Wez's eyes got round like saucers. He pointed

his finger at me and then growled, "You! You can run.... but you can't hide!" He froze with that threatening look, then broke out into a grin and started to chuckle.

We all ordered huge plates of breakfast and dug in.

"When we get back to the clubhouse, there's something I wanna bounce something off you, Sam," Ratchet whispered in my ear as I bit a fork full of scrambled eggs.

I stopped chewing. A flush of warmth crept up from my chest to my neck. What did he want to talk about? I wasn't going to share anymore with him about my time spent with the Hell Hounds. But I feared that my time was up at the clubhouse. I'd paid my debt to him.

The tab was paid. We got to the bikes, grabbed our helmets and shades off the handlebars and strapped them on.

"Sam, get on Gunner's bike and go with him," Ratchet said low to me and that's when I heard them.

The rumbling sound of pipes coming around the corner. Tweek and Rusty saw me. I strapped on my helmet and Gunner was already waiting for me to hop on the back of his bike. He was just starting his ignition as Rusty yelled out to Ratchet the moment they came to a stop only a few yards from us.

"Hey, Chaos. That piece of sheep tail doesn't fuckin' belong to you."

Ratchet walked toward them but turned back to

us, "Go. *Now.*"

Gunner had already released the clutch and we were out of the lot, Wez following close behind.

I was numb with fear riding with Gunner out of town. I feared for Ratchet. I knew the Hell Hounds and how they handled things. With verbal threats and physical violence. Ratchet was alone. Gunner and Wez were with me. They should have been with him.

We didn't go back to the clubhouse. They rode me down a secluded gravel road instead. We came to a clearing and there stood a single two-story house surrounded by trees.

"This is Ratchet's house. I live here too. In the basement. He was going to ask you today if you wanted to shack up here for a while. He thinks you might feel more comfortable here. Get you out of the clubhouse for a change... a good change..." Gunner steadied the bike as I got off.

Ratchet wanted me to stay here? At his house? My jaw dropped as I stared at the massive house with the white siding and brown shutters, all the trees surrounding us.

"I'll show you around... Me and Wez got a text from Ratchet. He's on his way here. He's ok, Sam."

"Yeah, I'm not leavin' till I see him for myself, brother. In one piece."

Wez stomped up the stairs to the front door ahead of us.

"It's my fault. I should have just gone with them. I caused all this. Now the Hell Hounds know I'm here with Chaos. They won't stop."

My heart was heavy and I started to shake. The dread. The fear. Swallowing me.

"You don't belong to them, Sam. Ratchet made that decision the night he brought you back to the clubhouse when those fuckers did what they did to you. Ratchet had a sadistic pig for a father. He was abused as a kid. Also watched his father beat his mother every other fuckin' week. Still feels like it's his fault and blames himself for what happened to her."

What happened to her?

I followed Gunner into the house and he showed me around. My mouth dropped open, taking in everything. Several bedrooms, huge living room and a cozy kitchen. Not too much home décor, but that's expected from two straight men living together. Two bikers for that matter. It was clean, considering, what I loved most was Ratchet's bedroom. The master bedroom with a king-size bed. Just two nightstands, some clothes scattered on the floor and a master bathroom, with a nice tiled shower that had glass doors.

I sat cross-legged on Ratchet's couch in the living room with Gunner and Wez. I fidgeted and watched the clock on the flat screen TV. Gunner took a few swigs from a whiskey bottle from the kitchen and passed it to Wez. Gunner scowled and kept tapping his foot. Wez kept getting up off the couch and pacing back and forth in front of me. I couldn't move. I focused on that clock. My mouth was dry. My throat hurt. I imagined horrible things Tweek and Rusty could and would do to Ratchet. And how I would never forgive myself if something happened to him… and for putting him and his brothers of Chaos Kings MC in the crosshairs of the Hell Hounds.

I jumped at the sound of the front door opening. Ratchet. In one piece. Before he could shut the door, I was already off the couch; both my arms wrapped around his shoulders and I held on. Tight.

"Whoa, Little Rabbit. I'm ok," his voice was deep and low against my ear.

I leaned back from his shoulder to look at him. His lip was bleeding. Rusty hit him. I was sure of it.

I let go and touched his cheek, "I'm so sorry… Sorry for dragging you into this."

He tilted his head. The side of his mouth lifted into a smirk. His eyes. His mouth. So male.

"You didn't drag me into anything, Sam. I made this my business. *You* are my business…."

He leaned down and kissed me quickly, softly. I tasted the blood from the cut on his lip.

"I'm sure Gunner gave you the tour of the bachelor pad. Go on upstairs to my bedroom, Sam. I'm gonna talk to my brothers for a bit and I'll meet you up there."

I sat on his bed and waited. Relief sunk in just a little and some of the tension eased off as well. I heard Ratchet's voice as he talked to Gunner and Wez.

Then his booted footsteps were heard coming up the stairs. He entered the room and I was off the bed to meet him halfway. I wrapped my arms around his waist and buried my face into his hard bicep. I breathed him in. Leather, sweat, cigarettes, wind. Ratchet. His familiar scent so comforting. I heard him inhale against my hair.

"Mmmm.. You always smell like sweet things, Sam… Not sure if its strawberries, but I like it."

He lifted my chin. I saw the bloody cut on his lower lip.

"Yeah. Rusty landed one punch," his tongue darted out to sweep along his lower lip. "That's all he got in. They were gone once someone called the law. I planned on bouncing the idea of having you stay here at my place instead of the clubhouse. But I guess we don't need to have that talk now, do we, Sam."

He bent down and kissed me again when I smiled up at him. I felt his grip on my hair as he slid his tongue into my mouth. Both our tongues flicked and mingled with the metallic taste of his blood.

I didn't want to let him go.

"I know you've had to survive through some really fucked up shit. I'm trying to be as gentle as I can with you, Sam. But sometimes, like right fuckin' now, I don't think I can… I don't think I ever can."

He released me, pulled his cut off and lay it on the bed and walked into his bathroom. I heard the shower come on and a few seconds of rustling to remove his clothes and boots. When I listen to the shower door close, I made my way in there. His back was turned to me; his head leaned back as the water sprayed his face. I stood there for a few seconds, admiring his broad shoulders and a wide back that tapered to a sculptured ass and thighs as thick as trees.

I began to take off my clothes. He didn't hear me until I stepped into the shower behind him. He turned around to face me. His lips were pressed tight together and his brow was set in a deep scowl. He reached up and raked his fingers to push away my soaked hair. Then he fisted his strong hand in my hair. His grip pulled my head back tilting to stare into his eyes.

"You're *mine*, Sam. You belong *me*," he growled low, but then suddenly let go.

"Turn around," he commanded.

I turned away from him. His hand pressed against my back, pushing me to bend over. I braced both hands against the tiled wall. The warm water splashed my back and my ass. I wanted to show myself to him. I widened my stance, stood on the tips of my toes and arched my back. I heard his deep moan and he seized my hip with one hand. He glided a finger in between my center, as his thumb rubbed my other tight hole.

"I want you, Sam. I want to mark you as mine."

I lost my voice. I was breathing hard and fast. I did want him to make me his and his *only*.

"Tell me. Sam. Tell me what you want."

"Yes... I want you," I answered, breathless.

"You want me to what, Sam?"

"I want you to fuck me, Ratchet. Please…"

He gripped my hips and braced his thick head up against my slippery opening.

"I'll give you as much of me as you can handle."

He slid into me slowly. He was so thick and heavy I was being stretched. But I wanted all of him.

"Fuck, Sam. Your pussy is so tight. Can you take more?" he gritted his teeth; voice strained.

"Yes, James. I need all of you!"

Slowly his thickness invaded me; stretched me. My walls wrapped around him so tightly. I gasped and keened. I was fully impaled. He moved his hips and withdrew slowly and slid all the way back inside of me. His pace was slow at first and I moaned feeling the incredible sensations he caressed deep inside me. I cried out when he grabbed a fistful of my wet hair and pulled.

His breathing was ragged and picked up speed with rhythm to his thrusts. His hips were smacking up against me, slapping sounds echoed off the tiled walls. I had to brace myself and splayed my hands on the wall as he drove into me faster, harder.

"You. Belong. To. Me!" he growled in beat with his ruthless thrusts.

"Yes, James!"

"Get ready, Rabbit. I'm going to fill you up. Right fuckin' now!" he roared as his liquid heat exploded deep inside me.

Our hearts raced, the shower spraying both of us. His hands came around and he pulled me up against his heaving chest. We stood frozen like this a moment. Our breathing was settling back to a normal pace. His lips and bearded cheek nuzzled my ear.

"My sweet, Samantha…" he whispered.

CHAPTER FIFTEEN

RACHET

I dried Sam off and carried her to my bed. I cradled her naked body close to me. She laid her head in the crook of my arm and fell asleep. With my cum deep inside her. I stared up at the rotating ceiling fan, listening to the quiet whirring sound.

I wanted Sam again. Sink myself deep into her again, but I had been too rough with her. I frightened her but doubted she would say so if I asked. That was all I knew when it came to fuckin'. I never had a problem getting my dick wet. If I wanted pussy, I got it. Mandi was fun for a short minute, but that's all it was. Fuckin'. Shootin' my load. And her begging for it. And calling me Daddy… Couldn't fuckin' stand it though!

How could I just take Sam so rough like I just did? That was all she knew herself. Things Sid and the Hounds made her do for so long. And I just did the same thing to her.

I left one of my t-shirts out for Sam to wear when she woke up. My back was turned, but I heard her bare feet pad into the kitchen. She must have woken up to the smell of bacon and eggs cooking. I was in front of the stove and turned around to look at her. She had that cute messy bed hair, wearing my t-shirt that was four times too big for her and hung down right above her knees. She combed her hand through her messy, dark hair and gave me a sleepy smile and yawned. My dick jumped in my sweatpants at the sight of her. I looked down at it. I was like a fuckin' a teenager with a boner every other minute the wind blows.

"Have a seat. Got some coffee brewed and breakfast cookin'."

"It smells so good," she stared at me, her head tilted a little.

"What? You never saw a man cook food before?" I smirked.

"Ah. No. Never."

"Well, now mark that off your 'must see' list."

I put a plate of eggs and bacon in front of her and when she finished it, she burped like she did when I took her to the Knotty Pine.

"Did you sleep good Sam?" *Probably not after what I did to her in the shower.*

"Yes, I did. I don't remember sleeping that good in a long time. No dreams either..."

"That's good... I want to apologize for what happened last night in the shower. I shouldn't have done that to you. I don't know gentle. And I don't want to add more of the bad for you. You deserve only good things."

Her head tilted. Her cute little eyebrows drew in together. Then she looked away.

"You didn't hurt me..."

"Yes, I did, Sam."

She pushed her chair away from the table. Getting up, she stepped away then stopped before spinning around, "I shouldn't be here."

"You're not leavin'."

"Just because you fucked me doesn't mean you have control over me, Ratchet!"

I was up off my chair. I stepped toward her then stopped. "You're not fuckin' leavin', Sam!" I came at her again. She backed up against the fridge. I slapped both my hands against it, caging her in.

"You're safer here than at the clubhouse."

She had to crane her neck to look up at me, her eyes glaring. Her lips parted.

I reached up and rubbed my thumb across her

pouty bottom lip. I wanted to pull it into my mouth and suck on it.

Her hands came up to press against my chest, "Stop. You're crowding me again!" She slipped under my arm and ran upstairs to my bedroom.

I didn't follow her. She needed her space.

I drove my truck to the clubhouse and bundled up her clothes into a duffel bag and grabbed her backpack from the room she slept in. On the way back, I bought her a pay as you go smartphone. I walked into my bedroom and saw her sitting on my bed, the covers drawn up around her.

"I brought back your things from the clubhouse. Also got you a phone. You should have one. I want you to use it, Sam." I handed her the phone and placed her bags on the floor by the bed.

"Just let me go, Ratchet."

I sat down next to her on the edge of the bed. "And where will you go? They know now you're with me."

"Then I'll just go back to Sid —"

I shot up from the bed, "Fuck, Sam! No. Not happenin'!"

I closed my eyes, shook my head and ran a hand through my hair before walking out of the room.

CHAPTER SIXTEEN

SAM

We didn't talk for the rest of the day. He gave me my space and left on his bike for a few hours. He was angry. Angry at me and probably wanted to clear his head. I laid in his bed all day. I closed everything off and huddled in that bed in my own world.

I could see the sun was just setting when I heard his bike pull into the driveway out front. His heavy boots were lumbering up the stairs to his room. When he appeared in the doorway, his hair was messy and windblown. I caught the scent of his leather cut and warm spring air.

"I want to lay next to you. That's all."

He walked in, peeling his cut off and laid it across the black wingback chair. He bent down; took only his boots off and slid into the bed under the blankets next to me. And we slept.

I woke up, my body racking with sobs.

"Shhh... I got you, Sam. Just a dream...," Ratchets warm breath whispered in my ear. His thick tattooed arm draped across my chest.

It was a dream. Not real. I'm here now with him. Safe.

"Sometimes I can't breathe. Sometimes I don't want to breathe."

"Tell me about it. The dream. Once you let it out, you'll realize it was just a dream."

"The things I dream about are real. They really happened to me and I relive them in my sleep."

"It's all in the past, Little Rabbit. You're here now. You need some good things to happen to you from now on. And those bad dreams will become less and less."

I stared up at the ceiling fan. "I didn't have a father growing up. I didn't know who my father was. Neither did my mother..."

He squeezed me just a little, rubbing his forehead against my cheek.

"My mother was a club whore to the Hell Hounds. Meth and money were all she lived and breathed for. I was her crutch. Her pawn. Sid's father, Knuck is the President. She made a deal with them. She left town with a good amount of money. And she left me with them. I was now their property."

Once it was spoken, I didn't want to stop.

"I did things, Ratchet. Bad things. I did what they told me to do. If I didn't, they'd hurt me. In all kinds of ways. I saw what meth did to my mother and some of the Hounds and I never touched it. The only way to numb the pain and the world I lived in for me was to drink, so I drank. Sid stalked me and claimed me as his property. Knuck was okay with that, as long as Sid kept me in line. I was used to pass drugs to club members that were locked up. I was prostituted out. Passed around to other men."

Ratchet lifted himself up over me, leaning on one elbow.

"My father was a monster. I did what I had to do to survive. But I didn't do enough for my mother."

"What happened to your mother?"

He turned away from me, squeezing his eyes shut.

"She committed suicide."

I reached up and pressed my hand to his cheek, turning him to look at me. "It's not your fault."

"Yeah… everyone says that. You say that. But I don't believe it. When someone you love takes their own life, you will always feel responsible."

* * *

"Why, Ratchet?"

"Why what, Sam?

"Why all of this? Why do you want to help me? I'm just a club whore."

"You are not a club whore. You were dealt a bad hand, Sam. Like me. Like my mother. I don't care what you had to do. But you survived. What matters is what you do now."

His mouth lifted in a lazy smile. His hair was messy. His chestnut color eyes so intense.

"It's a good day to ride. Do you want to ride with me, Rabbit? Just us? I want to show you what I found yesterday."

* * *

Ratchet was right. It was a beautiful day for a ride. Just the two of us. The strong wind was pushing against us both. The vibrations of the bike seat were felt on my ass and thighs and his male scent was intoxicating.

He pulled into a parking lot in front of a used bookstore. In the window were displays of books and a Help Wanted sign taped to the front glass door.

"Hop off, Rabbit. Let's stretch our legs for a bit."

Ratchet lit a smoke while I unstrapped my helmet.

"Why did we stop here?"

He exhaled his first drag.

"I saw that Help Wanted sign there yesterday when I was out riding. Thought you should go in and apply for a job."

I could see a young woman behind the counter, ringing up a customer through the glass window.

"I have only waitressed and bartended. That's about the only work experience I have, Ratchet. Look at me."

His eyes roamed down my body and his lip lifted, "I *am* looking at you, Sam. And I like it."

I huffed at him shaking my head.

"Doesn't hurt to try, Sam. Go on in there and tell that clerk you want to fill out a job application."

"Oh, that easy, huh?"

"Yeah, Rabbit. That easy."

Sometimes he acted all smug. Pushing my buttons. I jutted out my chin to him, unzipped my jacket and walked in.

High bookshelves in rows, displaying sections: Romance, Horror, Classic Literature, History and Children's Books. Storefront displays of popular and bestselling books, all *used* of course, with the creased spines. And then the scents of the store hit me, bringing back memories of my high school library — the dry smell of paper and cardboard. A few customers had a book in their hands, reading, flipping the pages. A girl that looked about my age, with purple colored hair was standing at the front desk, ringing up a customer on a cash register that looked as if it was purchased back in 1908 when the store opened.

I stood in line behind the customer that was paying the clerk with the purple hair.

"Thanks! Come again and remember that we give you a trade-in credit for any books you bring in."

She smiled as I walked up.

"Hi! How can I help you today?"

I smiled back and opened my mouth, "Hello, my name is Samantha. I saw the Help Wanted sign and I would like to apply for the job."

"Sure! One of the store clerks quit yesterday and I'm helping out working both shifts."

She reached under the counter before handing me a job application.

"Have you ever worked retail?" she asked as I looked down at the application. Must fill in the blank lines....

"Sam. You can call me, Sam. No. But I have worked as a waitress before." I didn't know if working at a strip club was something you would want to put on your job application at a bookstore.

"Well, it's all the same, Sam. Waitress, clerk, it's all in the customer service business. My name is Katrina. Well, everyone calls me, Kat. Pleased to meet you."

Kat looked out the big storefront window at Ratchet standing so confidently, hand in his pocket.

"If your friend wouldn't mind waiting, you can fill out the application now and I can give it to my manager later tonight when he comes in to help with my shift."

Ratchet looked at us through the window. He nodded his head and gave me a thumbs up.

Fifteen minutes later, I was trying to keep my lips tight as I left the store. It was no use. I was happy and he was grinning at me. My heart skipped a beat. Then his smile faded; his eyes were soft.

"With that smile, you can get a job anywhere, Sam."

* * *

A few hours later, back at the house, the store manager called me on my new cell phone and offered me a part-time job with some hours during the week and some weekends. I thanked him many times during the call and Ratchet caught me around the waist as I jumped and wrapped my arms around his neck.

"I got the job!" I squeaked against his ear

"That's fuckin' awesome, Sam," he mumbled low in my ear. His warm hard chest was pressed up against me. I realized then why his voice was so low and deep because I could feel it too. That warmth was spreading from my nipples to my stomach.

I heard him inhale as he held me tight against him, "You always smell so sweet."

I wanted to feel his lips against mine again. But I knew he wouldn't kiss me after what happened in the shower. I gave myself to him when every man I knew took it from me. But that deep yearning between my legs was relentless. I was too easy for him. I gave it up too easy for Sid and others.

He released me. "Congrats…," he said in a soberer voice.

* * *

My first week at my new job went quick. I met with the store manager, Miles my first day. He was a middle-aged bald man, dressed in the business casual of khakis and button-up shirt. We went over my job duties, which included stocking the bookshelves and training with Kat on how to run the register as well as help open and close the store. Kat was fun to work with and a good teacher. Books were categorized into groups: Romance, Horror, Westerns and then alphabetized by author's last name. I caught on quick and by the end of the week, I had re-stocked some of the shelves with more used books that were traded in by customers for store credit.

We would take turns at short thirty-minute lunch breaks to work the register and eat sub sandwiches we bought next door at the deli.

Ratchet rode me to the bookstore in the morning and picked me up after he was done with his shift at his job. He'd ask me how my day was and what new things I learned. He paid attention and listened to me as I talked, making me feel that I mattered. That I was *important* to him.

It was Friday night and Ratchet picked me up on his bike.

"Some of my brothers want us to meet up at the country fair tonight." He didn't look like he was too excited about it.

"Have you been to a country fair, Rabbit?" He turned to ask me as we left the bookstore.

"No. Never been. Heard it could be fun though."

"Well, let's do this then."

Ratchet smelled clean and fresh from a shower and along with it, leather, cigarettes and his natural male musk. I inhaled deeply and held on, wrapping my arms around his waist. Sometimes I buried my face in his back and closed my eyes, relishing all of it: him, the air pushing against us both, the loud rumble and vibrations of his pipes.

We met up with Gunner, Wez and Magnet with an attractive woman draping her arm over his broad shoulders.

Chaos walked together, stopping to play games like popping balloons for prizes, shooting pellet guns at paper targets and the strong man game, where Ratchet and Gunner took their turns slamming a huge mallet down on a podium that made the bell strike the top of the scale blinking 'Winner! Tough Guy! Strong Man!'

I smelled all kinds of delicious things like popcorn, cotton candy, funnel cakes, hamburgers and hot dogs cooking. It was just after sunset, lights from the rides and the games came on. Kids ran around laughing, or stood in line to get on the Ferris wheel, Tilt-A-Whirl, Octopus, or the Bumper cars. Screams were heard on some of the rides from young children and teenagers.

I walked along with Ratchet, carrying the soft and fluffy pink elephant he won for me at the BB gun target shooting game. As we walked, he had a finger in the belt loop on the back of my jeans.

We came up to the Night of Terrors haunted house ride. Little wheels on wooden carts with benches sat on tracks lined up, facing a pair of wooden doors that opened from the inside, beckoning the next cart to enter the darkness. The other rides were more exciting to the teenagers, so a line was formed for this one. Ratchet stopped and watched a young boy sitting in a cart with his mother. He looked nervous, his little shoulders tight, his tiny hands gripping the handrail in front of him. His mother wrapped an arm around him. She smiled and said something to him that neither of us could hear.

"You wanna ride?" his eyes never left the boy.

"Sure. I'll ride this one with you."

"Well, let's do this then."

He told his brothers to go on ahead without us. He took my hand in his and I followed him up the steps to the wooden carts. Ratchet handed some tickets to the carny and he got in a cart. I sat down next to him and the carny lowered the bar rail that held us in. He was so wide that my thigh was pressed up against his.

"My mother took me to the county fair when I was a kid. Just like that kid ahead of us. We rode the haunted house ride together. Just like this one. I was scared shitless! But I remember my mother putting her arm around me. Telling me not to be frightened; that she would protect me from the monsters… The sad thing is she couldn't protect me from the monsters. And I couldn't save her from him."

He said it like he was talking to himself, remembering it.

The cart jolted and started to roll through the doors as they opened into the darkness. It was humid in the dark and smelled of sweat, rotting wood and wet things. Suddenly a neon green Frankenstein manikin lunged out of a closet to my left. I jumped and leaned into Ratchet's side. He reached up, lifted my chin.

"I can only imagine what you've been through and survived, Sam. I don't even *want* to imagine. But from here on, I will protect you. I will never hurt you. I want you to trust me."

There was a chill in the evening air, so he wore a red and blue flannel shirt underneath his cut. The sleeves were haphazardly rolled up past his muscular tatted forearms. He released my chin and unbuttoned his shirt showing a patch of dark chest hair that trailed down his muscular abs.

His arm came around behind me, laying it on

the back of the cart. He leaned his other forearm on his side of the cart but kept his eyes intently on me.

"I want you to trust me. I want you to touch me. You have control, Sam. Touch me anywhere and I'll show you. Show you that you can trust me."

I reached up and placed my hand on the nest of dark hair on his chest. It was hard and heat radiated from him.

"You have soft hands, Sam," he said in a low, strained voice, keeping his eyes on me.

My stomach fluttered from the sound of his voice. My hand glided down toward his nipple and it hardened at the touch of my fingers. He sucked in a breath and closed his eyes.

My eyes roamed down his body saw the shape of his hardness pressing up against the front of his jeans.

"See what you do to me, Sam?"

My hand left his hard nipple and wandered down further to his hard stomach and I felt the muscles tighten. I traced my fingers lightly over the bulge beneath his belt. He moaned.

"I want to touch you this way too, Sam. Gentle. But I don't know how. I've always been rough."

But he *was* gentle with me. He had been since the first night. He stopped when I was frightened. He quit when I wanted him to.

"I'm not afraid of you, Ratchet. I trust you…"

"Then kiss me."

I leaned into him and smashed my lips hard

against his. I didn't wait for him and my tongue dove into his mouth first, twirling around his. My hand stayed where it was on top of his hardness and I rubbed the palm of my hand over it. His hips rose from the seat to grind against my palm.

Silky warmth started in my nipples, hardening them. It spread down to my stomach and further down to between my thighs. I needed something. I ached for him to touch me. He pulled back from my hungry mouth.

"I want to touch you back, Sam. Let's show each other gentle," his voice was low and strained.

I nodded and replied, "Yes, Ratchet. Touch me."

His arm wrapped around me. His breath was shaky as he placed his other big hand on my stomach. He slowly unbuttoned my jeans and slid the zipper down. Moving his hand down into them, his middle finger slid in between my wet folds and deep inside me. I sucked in a breath. Dizzy, head spinning.

"You're so soft... So wet.... Does that feel good, Sam?"

I couldn't speak. I was breathing funny and my hips began to move on their own, rising to meet his finger as it slipped in and out slowly. I could only nod again and a sigh escaped my lips.

"This is how it should feel. I only want you to feel good. The way you make me feel when you touch me. The way you're touching me now."

I moaned. My breathing fast as his soft touch

against my wetness moved just a little more quickly.

"I love the sounds you make. You make me so fucking hard it hurts."

I was jolted back to my surroundings when he withdrew his finger from inside me. He brought his wet finger up to his nose and sniffed.

He slipped his finger into his mouth and sucked, "Mmm. Your scent. And you taste just as good."

The sounds of teenagers screaming and laughing came to us as we neared the end of the ride.

"Shit. The ride is over," he grumbled. He reached down; zipped up my jeans, then gave me a quick peck on my nose.

"It's getting late. Let's go back to my place. Did you have fun?" He buttoned his shirt closed.

"Yes, I did," I replied, beaming up at him.

His eyes widened and he grinned back, "There's that smile."

I held on to him tight as we rode back to his house. Ratchet kicked his stand down. We took our lids and shades off. He stepped up to me and planted his lips on mine. I moaned and stood up on my toes to wrap my arms around his broad shoulders. Suddenly his strong arms were around me, lifting me off the ground. My head was swimming as I felt weightless. I was floating and liquid warmth spread through my body.

His mouth trailed kisses along my jaw and down my neck, sending goose bumps to rise and my nipples hardened and ached.

"I'm going to finish what I started on that ride, Sam."

He set me down and took my hand as I followed him to his bedroom. My heart pounded in my chest as we climbed the stairs. Once in his room, I slipped my jeans and boots off. I stood there before him in only my tank top and panties. His eyes roamed down my body as he took off his cut, placing it on the chair, then unbuttoned his flannel shirt. As it fell to his feet, my eyes took in the sight of him.

His broad shoulders and arms were covered in intricate ink designs in various colors. A line of dark hair from his hairy chest led down the middle of his hard stomach and disappeared underneath the top of his jeans and black leather belt. He towered over me, but I was not afraid.

I slid in under the blankets, as he took his boots off, leaving his jeans on. He followed me onto the bed. He propped himself on his elbow, looking down at me. His eyes were calm, as he lightly traced his finger across my forehead to the side of my face and down to my chin.

"So pretty…," he whispered.

He leaned down and his tongue entered my mouth again. I felt his hand slide down my ribcage to my breast. He rolled my hard nipple between his finger and thumb, twisting it lightly. I arched my back, wanting more of his touch. I broke the kiss to catch my breath. He pulled my top down and I felt the air on my nipple as he exposed it. A jolt went through me as his warm wet mouth latched on and sucked, twirling his tongue around the hard pebble.

Sucking and licking my nipple; his hand roamed down my stomach. I gasped as it slid underneath my panties. His finger glided up into my folds and then went still. He continued to rub me on the outside, against my swollen nub.

"You're so wet... slippery."

I cried out as his finger slid all the way inside.

"Yes, Sam... let it out. I want to see you, feel you. Watch you come for me..." he growled as he drove his finger in and out.

Suddenly I felt tingling sensations all through my pussy. My breaths faster, almost panting.

"Please, James... What are you doing? It feels so good..."

"I'm gonna make that sweet pussy explode..."

His finger did not let up, bumping to meet every thrust.

The pad of his thumb began to rub my clit making small soft circles and suddenly something within me exploded. I arched my back and cried out his name. I clenched around his finger and rode off a cliff of ecstasy.

Once that wave calmed, my eyes fluttered shut. He slid his finger out and sucked on it, tasting me again.

"Mmm.... My sexy rabbit. Get some rest now," he whispered as I drifted off sleep.

CHAPTER SEVENTEEN

SID

I snorted a bump of coke, giving me another edgy high, letting what Rusty *just* told me sink in.

"I got one lick in and bloodied his fuckin' lip. Had to scoot, though. Someone called the 5-0."

I took another drag off my cigarette, watching the blonde dancing in one of the cages at the Steel Cage strip club. She was pretty enough, showing off to me by turning around and twerking to make her ass jiggle. I had her once to suck me off, but the bitch couldn't keep my dick hard long enough. And I needed to bust a load after knocking Sam out cold that night at the Crow Bar. She talked back to me like a mouthy cunt.

Twice now she ran off with those Chaos motherfuckers. Chaos Kings have been around this county as long as the Hell Hounds, with one exception: they weren't a diamond club, a one percenter club. I was the Vice President of the Hell Hounds, someday taking the gavel from the President, my dear old dad, Knuck.

I learned by example from Knuck. Bitches existed in this fucked up world for the sole purpose of being prostituted out, passed around, used and do other miniscule things, but risky illegal activities to help the club. If a gash got pinched by the law, it was low risk and not much of a loss for the Hell Hounds.

The moment I saw Bonnie's raven-haired daughter, I wanted her. And not only did I want her, but I also wanted to touch her, hurt her. I had a hard-on for a week the day she skipped town with some cash Knuck gave her. I couldn't wait to get my hands on Sam. Her dark hair and petite body all for the taking. That night she became the property of the club and it was a celebration. I got her first. She was so fresh and soft and innocent. But I couldn't deal with the defiant look in her eyes even as I smacked her around some and made her suck my cock. Especially with my cock hanging out in front of the whole club. That first hard smack on her soft cheek just made my cock harder. No way I would look like a pussy in front of the Hell Hounds. Not when I was going to be VP soon.

She learned quick, once I was done with her and then passed her around after. Sam did as she was told and I was proud of myself, proving to Knuck that I was ready to lead as VP.

I didn't know what got into her to think she could run off and leave the club. She made me look bad at Bike Week. Rusty chuckled, but Tweek didn't dare. Both were pieces of shit, but they were good partners when it came to making deals for the club. She paid for it when I found her walking alone down the coastal highway. Dumb bitch. At least she pocketed five hundred from Chaos.

The news Rusty just gave me made me see red. Of course, she's with that mother fucking Chaos again! She was staring at him like a bitch in heat the minute he walked into the Crow Bar. They both made me look bad. Look weak. I now feared I wouldn't gain the respect back that I knew I deserved.

"I told the Chaos pussy that the whore didn't belong to them. What do you wanna do about it?"

I shot out of my chair, my hand gripped Rusty's neck like a vice as I slammed him up against a mirrored podium.

"*This* is what I'm gonna do about it you dumb fuck," my eyes wide, teeth bared, an inch from Rusty's face

"I'm gonna squeeze that Chaos piece of shit's neck just like I'm doin' to you right now." I let go.

Rusty bent over, coughing, hand to his throat.

"Jesus fuckin' Christ, Sid!"

My face was red; lips flattened, eyes glared. I ran my hands through my dark spiked hair. Sam was my property and those Chaos motherfuckers were going to pay.

"Tail that motherfucker. I'll have a talk with Chaos soon enough."

CHAPTER EIGHTEEN

SAM

Saturday morning the Chaos Kings held their fifth Annual Poker Run, a charitable event that donated all proceeds to help the local Homeless Shelters in the county. It was open to the public, bikers and other MC's that wanted to participate and contribute to the cause. The starting point of the Run was at the Crow Bar where all bikers met at 10 AM and chose their first card from a card deck. Groups rode out and followed the route mapped out to local restaurants and businesses to draw another card. The end stop was back at the Chaos King's clubhouse where local vendor tents were erected outside in the lot and various local bands performed, with raffle ticket prizes being given away.

Kat was a saint for working my Saturday shift, so that I could ride with Ratchet on the Poker Run. Wez rode his bobber up the driveway and Gunner was just starting his bike up as Ratchet and I got on his Night Train. They all kicked their stands up and road together to the Crow Bar. It was a chilly morning. My muscles tightened to fight back against the brisk air and I hugged Ratchet tightly with both my arms and thighs. He reached around and wrapped his hand underneath my left thigh as we sat idle at the stop light.

He turned his head toward me.

"We'll be at the Crow Bar soon enough and I'll get you warmed up," he said above the vibration and rumble of the bikes.

We arrived in time and gathered in the lot with Ratchet's other brothers in the MC. Tanya was the first friendly face I recognized among the crowd of bikers in leather, jeans, bandanas and shades.

"Sam! Ratchet told me you got a job at that bookstore! I'm so happy for you!" She squealed in my ear as she gave me a tight, warm hug.

"Thank you, Tanya. He's the one that pushed me to go in there and apply for the job."

"He got you there, but it's all you, Hon'!"

She was so openly warm and made me feel

welcomed. And having Ratchet there with me, I felt safe and protected.

Ratchet lightly tugged on the back of my jacket. Leaning down toward my ear his voice low with a smile, "Let's get you and Tanya inside and something to drink to warm you up."

I sipped on some warm cocoa, looking around at familiar faces. Magnet came over and gave me a friendly hug, then backing away with his hands up, telling Ratchet he was just being friendly. I guess he was *still* put out about the smile I gave Magnet at the clubhouse party.

Madge was there with her husband, Rocky, the Prez. They both received hug after hug from fellow club members and other MC's and bikers. Madge was all dressed up in her sassy retro style; red lipstick landing smudges on biker's bearded cheeks. Rocky doled out hard slaps on bikers' backs along with hugs and warm welcomes to some he hadn't seen all year.

I looked at the pool tables and remembered the night Sid left me out back unconscious, his temper flared and he lashed out at me. All because I noticed Ratchet walk in. An anxious warmth swam up from my neck to my cheeks. I shut my eyes. Snapshots flashed in my head. The images were of Sid and other Hell Hounds with their hands on my body. My thighs. My breasts. Their filthy dicks in my mouth. My knees scraped from the concrete floor in their clubhouse. Their laughter. Cussing. Calling me horrid things like whore, cum bucket and trash.

My eyes shot open to the sound of Ratchet's snapping fingers in front of my face.

"You ok, Sam? You had that look. Scared like you're ready to run."

The brows drawn close together made him look angry, but I guessed he was only concerned.

"I'm ok... Sorry, I just zoned out for a second."

"Nothing to apologize for. Do you feel weird about this place?"

I looked down at my hot cocoa in the Styrofoam cup, nodding my head.

"Don't worry. You're among my tribe, remember? I'm here. You're safe."

Rocky came into our space and I gathered myself and smiled at him. He gave both of us a brotherly bear hug.

"Gotta minute, Ratchet?" Rocky's eyes were smiling, but the rest of his expression was not.

"Yeah, Prez. Of course."

"Hang with Tanya for a bit, Sam," he said to me with a wink.

I watched as Ratchet followed Rocky toward the pool tables. Their conversation didn't last long, but both looked concerned, heads close so no one could eavesdrop if they wanted.

I went over to talk with Tanya at the bar. I didn't know half the people there and it was becoming a little overwhelming for me. I had been around bikers and MC's all my life, but now it felt different from what I was used to. Before Ratchet and the Chaos Kings, I was unnoticed, unless Sid made it otherwise. Conditioned to stay quiet and do as he said. Now, I'm free of him. People here looked at me; smiled at me.

CHAPTER NINETEEN

RACHET

"I should have heard about this from you, brother. Not from Gunner," Rocky said low for only me to hear as we stood together by the pool tables.

"Sorry about that, Prez. I just didn't want anything to blow back on Chaos. Making Sam my business is something I just gotta do."

"When you make something or someone your business, it *does* affect Chaos. Whether you're a rouge or not."

I raked a hand through my hair and nodded at Rocky. For every action, there is a reaction. Not sure why I thought Chaos would not be affected by my actions to bring Sam into our tribe.

"The word's out. The Hounds know Sam is with you now. They can run their mouths all they want, about how Sam belongs to them cause its bullshit. Maybe she was before you found her. But she's protected now. By Chaos."

"Thanks, Prez... Sam is a brave gal. She's a survivor."

Prez reached out, grabbed the front of my cut and bumped my shoulder into his, with a hard slap on my back.

"Let's go ride, brother. Drink a few later at the clubhouse and hopefully get some tail!"

* * *

We rode out with the MC's road captains, two to a group. Road Captains stopped traffic at intersections to keep the group together as we made our way to each stop for the poker run. Both Gunner and I served as road captains for the club, but I skipped out on it today since Sam road with me. Being road captain can be dangerous when drivers don't see us at intersections. I didn't want to put her in any dangerous situations that day, so, other members filled in for me.

Temps warmed up as the sun rose higher from

morning into the afternoon. We stopped in at local restaurants and bars to pick our next poker card. Thoughts of Sid and the Hell Hounds kept nagging at me. I tried to keep them out of my head and focus on Sam. Riding on my bike; her little warm body snuggled up behind me and her thighs hugged my hips. Her body moved with mine. When I leaned my bike into a curve, she leaned with me.

We were the first back to the clubhouse. There were a few vendors who had their tents set up, displaying what they specialized in selling – leathers, patches, bike parts, helmets and other things that appealed to us bikers. A wooden stage was built inside the clubhouse with the first of many local bands setting up and doing a sound check. The smell of hamburgers and hotdogs floated in the air around the parking lot from the grills set up outside.

I sat with Sam at the bar in the clubhouse, finishing off my second beer as she was halfway through her first one. Her cheeks were rosy pink from the wind. Her dark hair was a bit messy from the numerous times her lid was off and then back on again. And she smelled like leather and strawberries too.

I lit a smoke taking a nice long drag. I kept my hands to myself all day even though they were fidgety and wanted to be all over her. Sam seemed to enjoy the ride and I didn't want to see that faraway look she had at the Crow Bar. I was sure it was memories of Sid and the Hounds. So, it wouldn't have made it better with my hands groping her too.

Gunner *just* pulled in with the group he rode with and grabbed a barstool next to mine.

"I hope the Prez didn't rake you over the coals too much, Ratchet."

He opened his beer bottle that one of the Chaos chicks working the bar brought him.

"No, brother. It's all good. Just still trying to let it sink in. I wear the patch now. Chaos has my back."

"You got that right dammit..."

Gunner tipped his beer to me and took a drink.

I turned to Sam on my other side. She had finished her second beer. I had no idea what her tolerance was, but I kept an eye on her. The first band on stage started playing their set with some covers of classic ZZ Top. Sam leaned in toward me, smiling. She lost balance and fell into my chest. I caught her. Then I heard her giggle. It was cute.

"Whoa there, Rabbit. Maybe a just one more for you, huh?"

"Yep..." she mumbled and leaned back up on her stool.

CHAPTER TWENTY

SAM

I used to have a better tolerance for alcohol, but after two beers, I felt giddy.

"Let's do a shot of something, Ratchet."

I looked at the shelf of booze in front of me.

"How about some Petron?"

He smirked, "You really think you can keep up with me, Rabbit?"

"Sure, I can. I'll show you."

I walked around into the bar and came back with the bottle of Petron and three shot glasses.

"Let's share with Gunner too."

I started to pour the tequila into the three glasses. Gunner shook his head but was grinning. We would have to do without the salt and lime. The three of us raised our glasses.

Ratchet toasted, "To a good ride today."

We downed the shot at the same time and slammed the glasses back down on the table. I wiped my mouth with my forearm, trying not to show my sour pucker.

"Another one, guys?"

"Not for me, Sam. Keeping an even keel today with the beer," Gunner turned down the next shot.

I poured me and Ratchet another and we shot it down together. I slammed the glass on the bar and I was suddenly off my barstool. I wrapped my arms around Ratchet's scruffy, bearded neck, giving him a smacking kiss on his cheek.

Just his scent made me wet between my legs. I inhaled deep and moaned into his ear. His big hands came up and grabbed my hips.

As I leaned back to look into his brown eyes, his stare was intense. He bit his lower lip and I saw hunger in his eyes. *Just* for me.

"I can't keep my hands off you, Sam. Then you tempt me even more when you moan like that..."

I sensed the struggle within himself. How he was trying so hard to be gentle with me, which made my pulse pick up speed.

"You're so small," he grumbled low; looking

down at his hands on my hips.

"I don't wanna hurt you, Sam."

"It only hurts when I don't feel your hands touching me."

His mouth suddenly crashed into mine. His tongue penetrated my parted lips and wrestled with mine. This time he moaned and gripped my hips tighter. I didn't hear the live music anymore. All I could hear, see, smell and taste at that very moment was him.

He broke the kiss suddenly, "I'm taking you back to my place. *Now.*"

Ratchet rode me back to his place above the designated speed limit and I felt alive. I leaned with him as we took the curves, the chilly wind on our faces. We parked the bike rushing to take our helmets off. He smashed his mouth into mine like he did at the clubhouse. He bent down and his cold hands grasped the back of my thighs, lifting me to wrap around his waist. My eyes were closed as I continued to tongue his mouth as he carried me to his house. My back was pressed up against the front door. He ground his hips against the front of my heated center.

He broke the kiss, "Fuckin' clothes! Gotta get you out of 'em, Sam."

I giggled, but I felt the same frustration. Our bodies joined at that moment, but the hindrance of clothes blocked what we both needed.

He smiled, still holding me, but I heard the

jiggling of his keys as he opened the locked door.

He carried me up the stairs to his bedroom, my legs still wrapped around his waist. Next second I'm standing with him, my arms wrapped around his broad shoulders, our bodies pressed as close together as possible. His warm lips and rough beard nuzzled my neck and shoulder. Goosebumps rose all over my body.

"I'm going to do things to your body, Sam. With my hands, my mouth and my hard cock...," he growled close to my ear. My nipples hardened and ached for his touch.

His tongue feasted on my mouth again as he unzipped my jacket. Pulling it off my shoulders and onto the floor; lifting my top and unclasping my bra, his hands cupped my breasts squeezing them. His thumbs grazed my nipples and flicked them back and forth, making me arch my back up to him. He lowered down and he drew one into his warm wet mouth, sucking and flicking his tongue against the hard pebble.

A jolt of heat ran through my body and I gasped and gripped his shoulders, hearing him moan against my nipple as he continued the pressure of sucking, twirling his tongue over and over. He released it with a sweet little smacking sound.

"Get on the bed, Little Rabbit," he said low taking off his cut and hanging it on the chair, stripping his t-shirt over his head.

I watched him unbuckle his belt, removing his

boots and lowering himself on the bed next to me. His mouth smothered me with kisses. His tongue darted out and trailed down my stomach.

I arched my back again and moaned. My nipples hard as pebbles, on display for him.

"Please don't stop, Ratchet."

"Not gonna stop, Sam... Not this time..."

He was suddenly on his knees above me, pulling my boots off and yanking my jeans down. He froze and his eyes roamed my body, devouring me.

"God, you are so beautiful, Sam. So real."

He planted warm kisses on my thighs, moving toward my hot and wet center.

"Has a man ever kissed you here, Sam?" He mumbled in between his kisses tormenting my thighs.

"No. Never," was all I could manage to say.

"Open yourself to me, Sam. I want to see you. Taste you."

I opened my thighs to him. He nestled his big body between them. His tongue darted out, down the middle of my opening, sending jolts of pleasure deep inside me. He caressed my body with his tongue and lips and the desire I felt was new and exciting. He opened my folds and began to flick his tongue across my little nub lightly. I raked both my hands through his hair, feeling the softness of it and the warm sensations of his mouth.

My hips rose off the bed moving with the rhythm of his tongue making little, wet circles against my clit. An orgasm suddenly exploded from me and I cried out, grinding up against his mouth, riding the wave of hot ecstasy.

I was sighing and keening, breathing fast. He lifted himself up above me. The head of his hard thickness was at the opening, between my pussy lips.

"I'm gonna be gentle this time," he gritted out low and strained.

Moving slowly, he entered me. His thick girth stretched me. He moved his hips gently and pulled out and then slid back in. My nails dug into his shoulders and back, crying out when he was totally deep inside. My hips rose in rhythm to meet his and I felt another orgasm rise and explode around his hard cock. My walls contracted around him tightly as he started to move his hips faster.

He pulled away and was on his knees above me. He gripped his wet hard shaft, pumping it fast. He roared, throwing his head back. I watched his milky, hot cum shoot onto my breasts and stomach.

I smiled up at him and sighed. He lowered himself back down to cover me again. I wrapped my arms around him feeling his heart pound against mine.

* * *

When Tanya called and invited me over to her apartment to watch a movie, I was so excited giddy for the next two days. I never really hung out with girls when I was in high school. I just kept my nose in books and studied. I envied them, in their cliques planning on what they were wearing to Homecoming or who was going to the Friday night football games.

Kat and I were working on the stacks of used books traded in at the counter, grouping them by genre before stacking them in the appropriate sections in the store.

Kat was filling me in about her weekend and how she went to see the latest movie with a date.

"The movie was pretty good. My date was not so…. He's nice and all and I've been out on a few dinner dates with him. But he doesn't really interest me. Like he doesn't have an edge to him."

She got quiet concentrating on the titles on the book spines.

"Sam?"

"Huh?"

"What's it like dating a biker?"

I turned to look at her. She smiled and a pink shaded blush came over her face.

"It's nice I guess. You know, Kat, bikers are no different than anyone else. There are good and bad ones."

"Please don't get jealous when I say this, Sam. I have only seen your boyfriend on his bike when he comes to pick you up. And I think he is so… I don't know… he looks like a caveman! A very handsome caveman!"

"Yeah. I guess Ratchet is in a way. He is kind of a primal in some ways," I giggled.

"Is he nice to you?"

If Kat only knew how I had been treated when I was property of Sid and the Hell Hounds.

"Yes. He's kind and gentle."

"Well, your caveman just showed up, Sam," Kat nodded her head toward the glass door of the store. Ratchet pulled up in his truck out front.

"Hold on. I'll ask him to come in, so that I can introduce you."

"Oh gosh, Sam! No. I'm so friggin' embarrassed now," she called out as I walked to the front door. I smiled at him sitting in his truck and beckoned him to come in with a hand gesture.

He got out of the truck and walked toward the door with his confident swagger. Walking in full stride, a playful grin on his face.

I met him at the door and tip-toed to speak low in his ear," My friend, Kat wants to meet you. Is that ok?"

"Sure, Rabbit."

We both approached Kat. Ratchet winked at her and gave her an easy nod.

"Kat, this is Ratchet. Ratchet, this is Kat."

"Pleasure, Kat," he reached down and took her hand in his huge one and gave it a gentle shake. Her eyes were round saucers as she looked down at her hand swallowed up in his.

"Ah… Hi, Ratchet"

He smiled at her turned from her gawking eyes to me.

"Ready to go, Rabbit?"

"Sure… I'll see you tomorrow, Kat."

"Ah… Ok, Sam. Have a nice night you two," she smiled at both of us as we left the bookstore together.

On the ride back to his place was when I told him about my plans with Tanya.

"Not sure it's a good idea yet, Sam. You and Tanya should just go and hang out at the clubhouse instead."

Ratchet sounded a bit annoyed.

"Why? It's just Tanya and me. She wants to watch a movie and talk."

"I just need to keep my eye on you. Don't want to give the Hounds any opportunity. Not on my watch."

I crossed my arms in front of me. I turned from him and stared out the window at the blur of trees passing by us at forty-five miles per hour.

When I talked back to Sid, I got a smack on the cheek and was told to shut up. I snapped out of that image in my mind and grounded myself back in the truck again with Ratchet. I was fed up with his hovering over me. I turned back to him.

"You're crowding me again. Sometimes I think you don't trust me. You think I'm going to run again, don't you?" That was my voice. And it came out loud and clear

He turned to look directly at me. His eyebrows raised and then the side of his mouth lifted in a smirk.

He huffed and chuckled arrogantly. Sometimes he acted smug and superior. He patted the bench seat next to him.

"Sam. Come over here."

I turned back to the window.

"No."

Suddenly we swerved off the asphalt, onto the gravel by the road. I lurched forward when he suddenly stomped his booted foot on the break.

"Look at me, Sam," he barked. I did.

"I'm crowding you? Get used to it. I know what those piece of shit Hounds did and *will* do to you if they catch a whiff that you're alone or not protected by Chaos or by me," his voice was strained. His brows pinched together with a look of anger and frustration.

"There's nothing left that they can do to me, James. I've been banged up a few times and the bruises have all healed now. I don't want to go back to that Hell. I'm leaving all that behind me. I'm doing good for me."

He shook his head and turned to stare at the dashboard. A few moments of silence between us.

"Ok, Sam. Yeah. You should go over to Tanya's. Do your girl night. But on one condition. You two stay there. Don't leave her apartment. And text me when you're ready for me to pick you up. Deal?"

My jutting jaw quickly turned into a smile.

"Deal."

He returned that handsome smile and patted the seat next to him again.

"Now come over here, Rabbit."

I scooted over next to his hard and warm body; my thigh pressed up next to his.

CHAPTER TWENTY-ONE

RACHET

I pulled into Tanya's apartment parking lot with Sam on the back of my bike. I was also keeping watch on my side mirror at the primer grey car that followed us a few blocks away. I parked and planted both feet to steady the bike as Sam got off.

"I'll be back later tonight to pick you up, Rabbit. Have fun with Tanya."

I kissed her juicy lips quickly to get her go up to Tanya's apartment quick. I watched her plump little ass as she walked away and up the stairs to Tanya's.

I let out the clutch and rolled on the throttle back out the lot and turned left. The grey car pulled out and followed. I kept it at the legal speed limit. It pulled up to my right side at a red light. I looked over. It was that Hell Hound. The same motherfucker who got a punch in at the Knotty Pine. He rolled down his window, turned toward me and pulled his shades down his nose.

"Hey, Chaos. My VP wants face to face. Like *now*."

"Lead the way, dip-shit."

The light turned green and I followed him a few miles. Ten minute ride and I pulled in to the lot at the Steel Cage strip club. Should have known this would be the spot Sid wanted to meet. I turned off the ignition and then swung my leg off my bike. The Hound got out of the car and walked up the steps. I took off my lid, lit a smoke and followed him inside.

It was dark inside the club, clouds of cigarette and cigar smoke floated around me. Black lights made some things show up bright like the tiny G-strings the dancers wore on the center stage and in the three cages in each corner of the place. Marilyn Manson's version of "Sweet Dreams" blared through all the speakers. The heavy beats thumped throughout the place and in my chest. I didn't see any customers, only a good number of Hell Hounds standing or sitting near the stage. I was outnumbered and I knew I would be.

Dip-shit Hound was three steps ahead of me.

He stopped and turned around to face me. I got another good look at him since the Knotty Pine. Reddish greasy long hair, pale eyes and a long beard. Tall as me but not as wide.

He chuckled right in my face. "That whore's pussy been fucked so much, you'll *want* to give her back."

I was just a foot from his face. He started to chuckle.

I grinned back. My left fist came up with a hard jab, connecting with his face in half a second. Surprise, mother fucker. I'm a southpaw.

I kept grinning as his head snapped back. He stumbled back a few steps grabbing his nose. He regained his balance and looked down into his bloody hands.

"We're even now, Hound." I couldn't stop grinning.

"You mother fucker!" he growled; charging at me.

The greasy fucker was quickly held back by another Hound.

"Cool down, Rusty. You'll get another turn. A dark-haired Hound held him by the upper arms. He looked a bit younger than me but looked able to keep the greasy Hound at bay and away from me.

"Get the FUCK off me Skully!" he jerked out of the other Hound's grasp.

"I'm off, brother."

Skully raised his hands up.

"You're going to have to give my property back, Chaos."

The voice came from a small round table near the stage. Sid. His silhouette, sitting in a wooden chair under the beam of a red stage light. Smoke hovered around his slender frame.

"Sam's not your property anymore, Sid. She's free but she belongs to me now."

He was off his chair, walking four paces toward me.

"Who the *fuck* do you think you're talkin' to, Chaos?"

"I'm talkin' to the VP and I'm tellin' you that Sam belongs to me now."

Sid rolled his eyes and tilted his head, "Out of all the gash out there for grabs, you want that little used up whore? Your club is not even in the one percenter business. She's worthless to, Chaos."

I was getting sick of hearing these pieces of shit dogs calling my Sam a whore.

"She's not a whore and never was. And now she's mine."

I turned and walked out of the club, anticipating the next move from any of the lowlifes.

"Hey, Chaos, enjoy that whore a few minutes more. She'll belong to me again in no time." Was the last I heard Sid spout off as I pushed on the metal door and walked out.

CHAPTER TWENTY-TWO

SAM

I really liked Tanya's apartment when she gave me a quick tour. The décor was bright and colorful, turquoise blues, orange and hot pinks.

"I just love your place, Tanya. The colors are so you," I said as she poured me a glass of white wine.

"Thanks, Sam. This place really needed a lot of colors after Matthew left," she smiled, but it faded the moment she said his name.

"I'm sorry, Tanya…"

"Oh, nothing to be sorry about sweetie. You

just have to learn from the hurt thrown at you."

I agreed with her. But that nagging worry came back to the forefront. Could I ever learn and move on past my pain?

"Come on, let's hunker down on the couch, sip some wine and girl talk!"

She handed me a wine glass and took my hand.

I was looking forward to spending some time with Tanya when she called me a few days ago inviting me over. She was kind and warm and had a happy glow to her.

"So, how do you like your job at the bookstore?"

"I really like it. And the other clerk, Kat, who works with me has been nice, showing and teaching me everything I need to know."

"The customer service business is fun. I like my job as a salon specialist. I enjoy making someone happy when they need a fresh look and I give them that new look. I can tell you like to make people happy too, Sam," she beamed one of her pretty smiles at me.

"I want to thank you, Tanya... For being kind to me. And helping me come out of my shell. I'm not used to having friends. I'm used to being around people who only want to take from me.... But then, maybe that's all I'm good for..."

I looked down at my wine glass, fighting the tears. She placed her soft hand over mine.

"Don't ever say that again, Sam. Whatever

those disgusting dogs did to you is not *who* you are. You know what I see? I see a *survivor*. A smart and brave raven-haired beauty. I can only imagine the hell you lived through. But you are here now. With me. With Ratchet. With the Chaos Kings."

I smiled at that.

"For the first time in my life, I feel safe, Tanya. Safe and free…"

"Yay! Good! Now let's get our drink on and watch a tough chick flick! Have you ever seen 'Thelma and Louise'? No? Well, you're gonna love it!"

We sat on her couch and she hit the play button on her remote.

The sound of three quick knocks came from the apartment door.

Tanya went to the door and looked through the peephole.

"It's Ratchet and Gunner."

She unlocked and opened the door. Ratchet's eyes immediately searched and found me on the couch as he came in with Gunner following him. His brow knitted together with a look of concern? Worry? Fear?

"Sorry for crashing your night. Came back for Sam to get her to the clubhouse. Gunner is hanging back with you, Tanya."

* * *

Ratchet rode me to the clubhouse above the speed limit. I leaned with him as he took turns and his thick body felt tight and bunched up with tension. He didn't say anything to me before we left Tanya's except to hold on tight.

As we walked into the clubhouse, I saw only Chaos. All members of the Chaos Kings MC were there; sitting at the bar, smoking and playing pool. Wez and Magnet were there and of course Spider the VP and Rocky the President.

Ratchet patted my rear and leaned down into my messy, tangled hair.

"Go on into the bedroom, Sam. I have to meet with the brothers. It's ok. I'll be there in a few minutes."

I nodded and smiled at all the Chaos who looked at both of us. They all stopped what they were doing and nodded back to us.

I went to the bedroom Ratchet chose for me to stay at what felt like so long ago. I couldn't sit. I paced back and forth alongside the bed, biting my thumbnail. That anxious warmth spread again from my ears to my chest. That feeling of fear, of drowning. Something must have happened between Ratchet and Sid. I could feel it as we rode to the clubhouse.

Fifteen minutes later felt like an hour. Ratchet's huge frame came through the bedroom door. He shut it behind him.

"Come here, Sam."

I ran and crashed into him. I wrapped my arms around his broad shoulders, nearly strangling him.

"Mmm... there's that sweet smell," he mumbled into my hair. Then he pulled me away from him.

"I just came back from the Steel Cage, Sam. Talked to Sid and told him you belong to me now. But I needed to get you back here safe. Gunner will stay with Tanya to make sure the Hounds don't show up at her home. She's ok with Gunner there.

I knew Sid would not give me up so easily. He was the VP of the Hell Hounds MC. I felt his hold on me just then. I would never be free of him. And now I just put everyone I care about in danger. Ratchet, Tanya and the Chaos Kings MC. These few weeks were just a taste, a tease. A taste of what it would feel like to be cared for, protected, loved. It was short lived. I knew that someday soon I would be living back in Hell again.

I came down on my knees in front of Ratchet. Looking up at him, seeing the alpha territorial look in his eyes, I began to unbuckle his belt and unzip his jeans. He reached down to grasp my fumbling hands.

"Sam, stop. You don't have to do that..."

"I'm not stopping, James. Not this time."

I tugged his jeans and boxers down and his already hard cock sprung free an inch away from me.

I cupped my hand under his balls and caressed them as my tongue darted out and flicked the head of his heavy shaft. His skin was silky smooth when I tasted him for the first time. His head rolled back and I heard him groan.

"Fuck, Sam… I think about this every day. Your soft pouty lips on me."

I felt him gather a fistful of my hair in his huge warm hand, but he didn't move. He didn't push me. He just stood there frozen, waiting to feel my lips and tongue.

I licked underneath his shaft from the head to his balls and back up again. A quiet little moan came from my throat. I swirled my tongue around the smooth head and took half his cock into my wet mouth.

He sucked in a sharp breath and exhaled through clenched teeth, as I pulled him away from my mouth and dove him back into it. I took as much as I could and his head rubbed against the back of my throat. My mouth was slippery wet and full of my saliva. My pussy was just as slippery wet as I worked his hard cock in and out of my mouth, caressing his balls that started to bunch up and tighten.

"I can't hold back much longer, Little Rabbit. I'll explode in your sweet, warm mouth."

His voice was strained as he watched my head bob back and forth, his hips moving to my rhythm. I applied a light suction with my mouth and tormented him.

Suddenly his fist tightened in my hair and warm thick cum shot against the back of my throat. I stayed determined, swallowing all of him as his juice pumped and squirted. He roared at the same time as he exploded in my mouth and made my pussy gush again with more wetness.

His breathing was shaky and a sheen of sweat broke out on his hairy forearms. He released his tight grip in my hair. His pulsing cock slipped out of my mouth and I looked up at him.

"Sam... My brave, beautiful, Sam. That felt so fuckin' good. So much more than I imagined..."

We laid together on the bed. I curled up next to his bulky frame and took in the scent of his leather cut beneath my cheek. His arm was wrapped around me; his breathing was steady again.

He pulled away from me and shifted his bulky frame to lean on his forearm and stared at my lips.

"The first time I saw you, I pictured those sexy lips of yours on my cock. Then I saw that dick-wad rub up on you, and that look on your face."

His hand reached up and his finger traced the side of my face and pushed a bit of my hair behind my earlobe.

"Then you shot out of that bar stool so fast... I chased after you... and caught my little rabbit. And here you are. With me."

The tenderness I saw in his eyes made my heart skip a beat.

"You are a survivor, Sam. You escaped your hell. And you belong here with me now. With Chaos."

He lowered himself over me, pressing his hard chest against mine. His tongue glided into my mouth. It wrestled slowly over and over against my own.

* * *

His breathing was steady against my ear as I lay there, my back pressed up against his warm chest. I slid out from under his arm draped over me. I got dressed and tip-toed out of the room and out to the open bay door to the clubhouse. The sun was just beginning to rise over the surrounding trees and a chill was in the early morning air. His brothers had all gone home late the night before, leaving just me and Ratchet alone here.

I hugged myself and closed my eyes, inhaling a deep breath. I held it for a few seconds and exhaled.

Every moment I spent with Ratchet made me feel alive. I could breathe. I was safe. Those delicious tingles he made me feel with his kisses and touch made me feel happy for once in too long a time. Or maybe even for the first time in my life. He didn't look at me like I was a used-up whore. A whore that had been violated. He never saw the bruises on my body, my face.

"Sam!"

I turned around to see him walking toward me; jeans unbuttoned, belt unbuckled and boots untied. He gripped my folded arms and squeezed.

"I'm ok."

"Don't ever fuckin' do that again."

His brows were drawn together.

"I just needed a moment to myself. Needed to

get a breath of air."

I was crushed against his hard-bare chest. He wrapped his arms around me and held me tight.

"You scared me this time, Rabbit," he grumbled against my ear.

I pressed my cheek against his chest, listening to his heart thumping fast.

"Well, long time no see, Nomad."

I thought he was talking to me, but I followed his eyes down to his feet. A grey cat rubbed up against his calf.

"Not sure why, but he came around rubbing on my leg like this that night I spent the night here with you. This is the first time I've seen him since."

The cat looked as if it had lived a long time fending for itself. A feral cat. I had seen feral cats come around the Hell Hound's clubhouse before. Most of the time some of the Hounds would shoot and kill them with bee-bee guns like they were playing some carnival game, making bets on which one they could kill.

"I think he likes you too. I'll be back. Let me find a can of something for him to eat."

I stood there looking down at the lone cat, as Ratchet walked back into the clubhouse. I didn't stoop down to pet it even though I wanted to. Ratchet came back with an opened can of food and placed it on the ground a few feet away from me. The cat walked over immediately and purred as it began to eat the contents.

"Never had any pets growin' up. But I never had a problem with dogs or cats. I admire them. They don't have sick evil intentions like us. They just adapt. And have the instinct to live. Breathe."

His voice was flat, monotone as if he was reliving something from his childhood.

He stood up suddenly

"So, I guess we can call him Nomad?" I tilted my head, smiling up at him.

"Yeah, let's call him Nomad. Now come back inside, Sam. I think he's got the right idea. I wanna rub up on you," his mouth lifted into a smile.

We left Nomad to his can breakfast and I took Sam back into the clubhouse. I gave her the reins. I gave her the control and she rode my rock-hard cock. She was so uninhibited, impaled on me, back arched, sweat glistening on her flushed little soft body. She gyrated her hips with greed and took what she wanted from me. And I gladly gave it to her. Her perky tits bounced as she moved above me. She moaned and cried out as her slick wet pussy spasmed around my shaft with her climax. And she brought me over the edge as I pumped my cum up deep inside her.

CHAPTER TWENTY-THREE

RACHET

Ratchet slouched in a wing-backed chair alone at the funeral home, dark blue necktie loosened. The funeral services were over and everyone had left. The only other person there was the funeral director. Ratchet stared down at his cell phone sitting on the coffee table in front of him, next to a powder blue box of tissues. It rang once and Ratchet snatched it up and pushed the receive button

"Hello, Grandma?"

"Hello... is that you, Son?" her voice was soft.

"Yeah, it's me, Grandma. It's James."

He heard her start to cry and sniffle.

Ratchet listened to the sound of loud pipes from several bikes pulling into the lot outside the funeral home.

"Oh, Son…"

"It's my fault, Grandma. I should have done something, Take Mom away. Protect her from him—"

"No, son it's not your fault. Don't ever say that again. She did the best she could, she loved you so much. You were her life."

Ratchet squeezed his eyes to stop the tears, but they sprung anyway and one ran down his face to his chin and dropped on his thigh.

"Now listen to me, James. I want you to come see me and we'll talk. I live on 2389 Henderson Lane. There are some things I need to tell you about your mother, James."

"Ok, Grandma. I'll come see you first thing in the morning."

"OK, Son. That will make your grandma very happy. I love you, James…"

"Love you too, Grandma… bye…"

He came through the door as Ratchet shut his flip phone. It was his father, dressed in riding boots, faded jeans and his cut. A little grey sprouted through his deep brown hair and long beard. He was a hulk of a man walking toward Ratchet with the familiar gate that was not unlike his own.

He came to a stop above Ratchet. His stance was wide and he looked down at him. When he pulled his shades off, Ratchet saw his own eyes looking down at him.

"I guess I didn't make it in time for the services, Son…"

Ratchet was off the wing-back chair, his forearm up against his father's burly chest and with a growl, pushed him up against a concrete podium.

"Get out!" he growled through a clenched jaw an inch away from his father's face.

James Senior grabbed his son by the biceps, suddenly realizing Jimmy was as strong as he was.

"Or what, son? You ain't no better than me. She coddled you, made you into a fuckin' pussy! That's why she couldn't take it anymore. Drove me away, drove everyone away..."

* * *

Sam hugged me tight with her soft thighs and arms as I rode her away from the clubhouse. I drove her toward the mountains and found a quiet spot next to a secluded winding road and kicked the stand down. The gurgling of water several yards in the woods could be heard as I walked Sam on a dirt path. We came to a clear water stream. The dirt path was the only giveaway to the secret little spot that only a few people knew about. A huge boulder was anchored off the edge of the stream.

"Let's sit here, Sam. We need to talk."

She sat on the rock first and I lowered myself to settle next to her. I didn't know where to begin. I looked at her pretty face, strands of her raven hair blew in the breeze. Those pouty, adorable lips. I placed my hand on top her small one.

"I'm a spitting image of my dear ol' dad — James Racette the first. I look like him. I sound like him. But my mother was a soft-spoken woman, couldn't hurt a fly. My father, on the other hand, was the opposite, he liked to hurt. Liked to beat me and smack me around when I was a kid. He called me a pussy every other week, said I wasn't a Racette. Both my mother and I were just a burden to him. We were the reason he couldn't hold a job for more than a month. My mom was also the reason he couldn't keep his dick hard enough... Yeah, he told me that on a few occasions too.

He'd leave us from time to time for months. Mom struggled and had help from friends. My grandmother was there to help whenever he was gone. But he'd always come back. New job, new clothes and a reason to take care of me and mom. We were all afraid of him. My grandmother would go away but made sure she left us with enough food and an apartment where a lease was paid in full for 12 months. My mom would get a job, but when he came back in town, he made her quit and tell her to forget any of the new friends she met. He was a Racette and he would provide for us.

When I was a teen, I got into small scraps and fought at school. I took out my anger and fear of him out on other boys my age. Trying to prove I was tough enough for him, a bad-ass Racette boy. I also got mixed up with selling weed and smoking it when I could, which helped pay for groceries or anything my mother needed.

I came from school one day and my dad showed back up at our apartment complex. He rode into the parking lot on an old shovelhead, along with five other bikers. They all wore the same cut as him. He was patched in with the Hammer Heads MC, a diamond club out of North Carolina. I knew a bit about MC's but not much.

My dear ol' dad found us and came to celebrate his patching in with the Hammer Heads. Once off his bike, he lumbered over toward me. He was still large and fearsome to me. He slammed a meaty fist into my shoulder, telling me I grew like a weed. Then he introduced me to his brothers. He wanted to see my mother. I followed him and his members up the stairs to my apartment. And I was full of dread. I'll never forget the look of defeat and emptiness in my mother's eyes when we walked in. He grabbed her around the waist and planted a kiss on her cheek bellowing out, 'Poppa's home! Time to celebrate with my new club brothers, Babe!'

They stayed for *five* nights. My piece of shit father kept my mother in her bedroom with him. Five nights I heard her cry behind her bedroom door and feeling that ache in the back of my throat, not able to stop him.

I didn't go to school those days. Just stayed with mom, ran out to score some coke and dope for Dad and his brothers. Didn't know what else to do, I thought maybe they would finally leave one day soon.

The fifth night, I came through the apartment door and saw my mother crying. He had a fist full of her hair, dragging her out of the bedroom. He pushed her down to her knees on the floor, still holding a fistful of her hair.

'Dumb, Bitch. Thinks she can make my son grow up to be a fuckin' pussy!'

The other fucking members chuckled, sitting on the couch and the kitchen table playing cards, smoking pot, doing lines of coke on my mother's little mirror they stole from our bathroom.

Everything turned red before my eyes seeing my mother on her knees. I came at my father with all I had. Both my fists gripped onto the front of his cut. I yelled at him to get the *fuck* off my mother, calling him a sick piece of shit.

I didn't see him let go of my mother's hair. His fist slammed into my temple with a powerful hook and I went down.

It felt like my head was being squeezed in a vise when I came to. First thing I heard was the muffled sounds of cries coming from my mother in the bedroom, then the sounds of chuckling and whooping from that bedroom too.

My vision cleared as I opened my eyes to that throbbing pain and saw my father sitting on the couch, snorting coke from my mother's mirror with a rolled-up dollar bill. He looked down at me as I got up from the floor.

I'll never forget what he said.

'Shouldn't have done that, son. Showin' off in front of my brothers, big fuck-up on your part. Look at you now. Nothing but a pussy. Hear your mom in there? Yeah, my brothers are having some fun with her now. She's always been nothing but a waste of my time. A burden. That's all bitches are, boy.'

I don't remember what else he said because next thing I did was push myself off the floor and headed straight for the bedroom door. I grabbed the knob, twisting it back and forth, kicking it, yelling, cussing that those motherfuckers were *dead*. Then I felt something pressed hard against the back of my skull. And I remembered the Glock he had shoved down the front of his jeans.

He told me I was not going in there and that I wouldn't like what I saw if I opened that door. I didn't listen to him and continued to slam my shoulder against the door. Then I felt a sharp pain in the back of my skull. He knocked me out cold with the Glock.

I then felt something wet splash on my cheek when I came to. My head was cradled in my mother's soft lap.

They had left after they were done raping my mother. I never saw him again. Until the funeral.

I went to see my grandmother the day after my mother's funeral. She did age some since the last time I saw her. She gave me one of her tight hugs, well as tight as a fragile little woman could muster for someone the size of me by then.

She told me that day that my mother was from a family of wealth, The Wilmington's, from South Carolina, a long line of plantation owners. She was kind-hearted and smart. Beautiful chestnut hair and light brown eyes. She liked to read books when she was young and hung out with other girls her age, chatting about what girls chat about; boys, books and school. But when she finished high school, she had a little wild streak in her. I guess she wanted to experience some of the things she read in books. She was at a friend's house for a slumber party and that's where my father first saw her. He was buddies with one of the girl's older brothers. I guess he put on the charm with her. He was a big guy, looked pretty much like me. He reminded my mother of some of the dashing rogue characters in the books she read and she fell head over heels.

She was innocent when it came to men though. She didn't date in high school. And she was easily influenced by my father and nine months later, I was born. Daddy dearest was all proud and happy since he thought he hit the lottery. He thought knocking up the rich girl was his ticket to her family money. Well, he wasn't happy for too long once my grandmother made it clear to him that he wasn't getting a fuckin' dime of the family money. After that, it was Hell. He took her away from her friends and her family. He moved her to North Carolina with me on her hip.

After what that piece of shit of a father and his club did to my mother, I packed what I could and moved us to another apartment in the next county. I got a job at a local gas station. The owner let me tinker on my old Sporty I bought for a few thousand bucks. I did what I could to make money. Sold some dope and other drugs. I just took care of my mother and myself.

A few years go by; we're doing ok. Mother kept in touch with my grandmother and we did what we could to have a normal life. But mother was never the same. She would shut down sometimes and withdraw into herself and not eat. She didn't get out of bed for days. She always worried about me and when I'd be home, worried he would come back and take me away, mold me to be just like him. I did and said all I could to try to convince her that I would always be there for her. I was working the night shift at the register at the local gas station when I got the call from her. Her voice was faint on the phone; I could barely hear it.

'Jimmy…' was all she said.

She didn't sound right on the phone. I locked up the gas station and high-tailed it to the apartment on my Sporty. But it was too late. I found her curled up in her bed, still holding the cell phone.

She took a hefty dose of both Xanax and Ambien. She got the scripts from a local physician to help her with sleep and nervousness or anxiety. I don't remember what I did for the next two hours, I guess I blocked it all out. I found myself sitting on the bed, cradling her in my arms. I took her cell phone and dialed 911 then my grandmother.

I left my grandmother's house with a signed check in my name for ten grand. I canceled the lease to the apartment and took as much stuff I could to the local thrift store. I packed clothes in a duffle bag, strapped it onto my Sporty and rode up the east coast from North Carolina into Virginia. I landed here in Stayford County. I cashed the check and got myself an apartment and a job at the Towing service; I could tinker with my Sporty again. That's where I met Gunner. He had just come back from his last tour in Iraq and he rode up on a Harley softail. It was his first day on the job. We started shootin' the shit and we rode. He showed me all the good roads. He invited me up to the Chaos Kings MC clubhouse. They had an all-weekend party. Lots of drinking, more than a few bong hits and the chicks liked to have a good time too. Gunner introduced me to all the members and I sensed a brotherhood. A tribe who lived alongside society. Not a diamond club. Members had legit jobs, families and really knew how to party; have a good time and ride. And the most important thing to me was that the men didn't treat their women like shit. I became a hang around at first and then moved into prospecting. Gunner was my sponsor. I was fully patched in after only six months and Rocky gave me a position as one of the Road Captains.

I told Sid you're free of him and the Hounds. You belong here with me now. I will do *anything* to keep you safe. Safe with the Chaos Kings. You're a very brave woman. You did what you had to do to survive that fuckin' hell. I believe you were put in my path that night at Bike Week. That even in this fucked up world we both came out of, despite all the chaos that surrounds all of us and fight our way through, we can ride through it. Lead our own lives. Just breathe and take care of each other."

I stopped then. Just to let what I said to her sink in. I needed to let it all sink in too. She stared at me, mouth in a straight line, but tears were getting ready to spill out from the corners of her eyes.

"When I was with Sid, he controlled my every move, my every breath. I can still feel him. Inside my head."

"Do you want what I want, Sam? Ride with me? Make our own choices and decisions?"

"Yes, Ratchet. I do. I want to breathe on my own. Ride with you."

My mouth collided with hers just then. Our tongues twisted and tasted each other. She suddenly withdrew and leaned away from me.

"We both know this won't happen. Sid will not let me go. And if you get in his way, he will hurt you, your brothers, or even worse. My running away has just made him angry, he's in a rage now. You have put yourself in his path to get to me."

"I'm getting you a bus ticket to North Carolina. I want you to stay with my grandmother. No one, not even Chaos knows where she lives. You stay with her for a while until I figure something out. My brothers will help me figure things out."

She leaned down and nestled her cheek against my chest.

"But for how long? Does your grandmother know anything about me? I don't want to put her in any danger…"

"I'm going to call her today. She is a good woman, Sam. She's been there for my mother and me when she could. Remember, my mother's family comes from generations of wealth. That's what my scum of a father always wanted. The money. Sid is just like him, it's all about money. Those kinds of men think money is what makes you King. Just promise me one thing, Sam."

"What's that?"

"My mother couldn't overcome the pain and her disgrace of what happened. That's why I believe she checked out. Promise me, if you venture down that dark road, that you bring me along with you. You feel like checking out because it's the only solution, you come to me. I will do everything in my power to help you, whatever it takes. Get you the help of a doctor, medications, anything."

"Yes, James… I promise."

* * *

Two days later, Ratchet dropped me off at the bookstore so that I could tell Kat my plans. I had one of his duffle bags packed with my clothes, ready for my trip to North Carolina.

"Kat, I need to tell you something and to let our boss know. I have to leave town for a while, Ratchet's on his way to get me a bus ticket now. I have my things packed and I'm leaving today. I don't know when I will be back, so I understand if I lose my job over this. That's all I can tell you."

Kat stared at me for a very long moment. Her jaw dropped open.

"You're scaring me, Sam…"

"It's ok, Kat. I want to thank you for all you've done for me. Showing me how things work and helping me around the bookstore. You helped me come out of my shell. I will always cherish our fun talks and all the giggles."

I suddenly fought the tears that were ready to spill and swallowed the pain in my throat. I threw my arms around Kat and embraced her with a tight squeeze.

"It'll be ok, Sam… You're going to be ok. You're fortunate to have a boyfriend like Ratchet. He will help you. I will help you. Mum's the word. I'll tell the boss you have a sick aunt you need to visit for a while. I guarantee you'll still have your job when you get back. Just please be careful…"

She hugged me back tightly as the bell on the front door jingled. I turned around to greet the customer. My heart thudded against my chest.

"So, this is where my sheep's been workin'."

Sid sauntered in grinning.

"Baaaha Baaaha!" Rusty followed behind, making that horrible sound. The third Hound, with the dark hair, I didn't recognize.

I turned back to Kat, "Don't say anything."

She followed my eyes to look down at my cell phone lying next to a stack of paperback books on the counter. Her eyes met mine and she gave me a quick nod.

By the time I turned back to Sid, he was just a few feet away. The only barrier keeping him from getting to me was the counter and cash register.

"How did you find me?"

"Well, you know Mandi don't you, Sam? She's been hanging out with the brothers and me lately. She was pretty pissed off about you suckin' on that Chaos cock that she was bangin'. Did you know she's a wildcat? Whoa, boy. Can that bitch suck cock and take it all up the ass? We got her broke in really good."

Mandi. The last time I'd seen her was at Chaos King's clubhouse. Heads turned to get a good look at her curves and sexy clothes she wore, then that image of her changed. She'd been used and passed around like I was. My image of her now was different, she looked broken, frightened.

"I'm impressed, Sam. This looks legit. Working at a bookstore, hangin' with the Chaos Kings, blowin' a few of them too I bet. They're not even a diamond club, you dumb bitch. That's not your style."

My knees almost gave out on me. Numbness spread throughout my body and blood drained from my face. He had a permanent grin on his face, knowing what he was doing to me.

"Didn't that Chaos tell you I'd be coming back for you sweetheart? Bet he's had enough of you anyway. Let's go. I'll get you your job back at the Steel Cage. Gonna have to figure out what we'll do with you."

"Ok, Sid. I'll go with you. Just let it go with Ratchet and Chaos. I've had my fun."

His eyes turned to Kat.

"Who is this juicy thang?"

"She just works here. She's a bore. I've had to put up with her."

He grinned at her, his eyes roaming over her breasts and then downward.

"Bet you rub your pussy thinkin' about guys like us, huh? Bet that juicy body of yours bruises easily too…"

Kat peeled her eyes from him and looked at me, terrified, "Sam?"

"It's ok, Kat. I'm going with Sid ok?"

She followed my eyes again back to my cell phone.

The sun just disappeared over the horizon when I got on the back of Sid's bike. We rode to the Steel Cage, Rusty and the dark-haired Hound riding staggered behind us.

CHAPTER TWENTY-FOUR

RACHET

I placed the stuffed duffle bag full of Sam's things on the passenger side of the truck when my cell phone rang. Her name lit up on the screen.

"Hey, Rabbit."

"Ratchet?" It wasn't Sam.

"Yeah? Who's this?"

"James, it's me, Kat. This guy Sid and few of his biker friends – they call themselves the Hell Hounds? They just left with Sam. I'm so sorry! I didn't know what to do! I was so afraid! I'm scared for Sam!"

That painful ache in the back of my throat suddenly choked me. I had to struggle to swallow it down.

"Not your fault, Kat. You did the right thing. Do you know where they took her?"

"I don't know ... Ah... He said something about a Steel Cage." I heard her sniffling and crying.

"It's ok, Kat. Lock up the store. Keep this phone with you. If they come back, dial 911."

I was out of my truck and back in the house hollering down the basement stairway

"Gunner!"

He appeared at the foot of the steps.

"Sid took, Sam. Takin' her back to the Steel Cage. I'm going there first."

"Comin' with you, Brother."

Gunner left my sight to grab his keys to his bike and a 357 revolver. I didn't own or carry but was seriously considering it now. Kickstands up within two minutes and we were out of the driveway, throttles twisted and pipes wide open to the Steel Cage.

CHAPTER TWENTY-FIVE

SAM

As I followed Sid into the Steel Cage, a big burly Hell Hound, who I think they called Hammer, lumbered out of one of the private rooms down the hall to my right. Mandi followed behind. Her right eye had a dark bruise. She recognized me and I recognized the look in her eyes, the same as mine. Humiliation. Defeat. Fear. She looked away from me and stared at the back of Hammer's legs. She planted herself on Hammer's lap by one of the little bar chairs up at the front of the stage where a blond woman was moving to the beat of Nine Inch Nails.

Sid wrapped his hand tightly around my upper arm.

"Come over here, Bitch. We'll sit with Hammer and the wildcat."

He planted himself in a chair next to Hammer with me on his lap. He reached up to hug my thigh and he squeezed. Hard.

"Mm... Still soft. Still pliable...," he mumbled against my cheek.

Hammer chuckled as his huge tattooed hand did the same to Mandi's thigh.

"Hot damn, Sid! This one here *is* a wildcat. Just like you said. She sucks a mean cock."

Suddenly Mandi's head snapped back as Hammer grabbed a fistful of her hair.

"I'm showing all the brothers that video I just shot of you chokin' on my big dick," he busted out with a loud chuckle.

Mandi didn't speak. She squeezed her eyes shut, her mouth tight and her jaw jutting out.

Bile rose up the back of my throat. I was too numb now to be terrified. Numb. Defeated. Alone. My throat started to feel constricted, tightened up so I couldn't catch another breath. And I wished at that moment I could just give up the will to breathe.

"Now don't get jealous, Sam, you suck cock good too. I'll pass you around from one Hound cock to the next. Hammer can make a video for us too,"

Sid jeered up at me.

"Whatever you want, Sid," was all I could muster.

He rubbed his stubbled jaw, pondering something inside his sick head.

"I'll save that show for another time. I'm giving you a break tonight. You'll work the bar. Hell Hounds are celebrating tonight. Our sheep have come home."

I didn't know how much longer I could keep the tears from falling. Sid's hands disgusted me. Then I pictured Ratchet's big warm hands touching me... his gentleness... his russet brown colored eyes gazing at me. The scent of smoke, leather and his own male musk brought images of wrapping myself around him as we rode his bike.

A broad-chested man appeared within my view. He looked like he could be old enough to be my father. He had very short greying hair, with light colored eyes and he was a wide man.

"This is Vik, he owns the place now. Vik, this is the sweet little lamb I was telling you about."

Vik's eyes roamed my face and body as he grinned down at me, shoving a half-smoked cigar between his teeth. He swirled his tongue around the wet end.

"Nice little lamb you have there, my friend, she will do good behind the bar tonight." Vik had a slight accent. He sounded Russian. He raised his hand toward me. Rubbed his thumb across my lower lip and grinned at me.

Sid pulled me back, away from his thick stubby thumb on my lip.

"Maybe I'll let you get a good taste of her sometime soon. But not tonight…"

I was off Sid's lap and he pushed me ahead to lead him to the bar. A couple of women worked, wearing bright colored tights and black halter tops.

"Don't you bitches fight over the tips."

I lifted the bar hutch, stepping through and shutting it back down in front of Sid. This gave me a barrier away from Sid. I didn't know how much longer I could keep from throwing up.

"It's Ratchet with another Chaos. Just pulled in," that dark-haired Hound that followed us back here yelled over the loud thumping music.

Sid turned toward me and glared. His eyes were cold.

"How did those motherfuckers get here that quick, Bitch?"

Kat. She called Ratchet the moment we left the bookstore.

"I'll tell him to go away," I stammered out.

"Yeah, you do that, Little Lamb. Going to sit back and enjoy this," he sneered, walking back to his chair next to Hammer with Mandi still on his lap.

Ratchet appeared out of the darkness through red and blue strobes of disco lights. He stalked toward me. With purpose. Gunner was right behind him. He moved quickly, passing through the cigarette smoke, between the bar tables.

Sid's Hounds stayed back. The dark-haired Hound turned to me and leaned over the bar

"Just tell him you're cool with this. Hounds don't give a fuck about you or him," he said as low as he could above the noise of the thumping music.

I nodded to him. He stepped away toward the other end of the bar.

Ratchet opened the bar latch and his powerful hands curled around my arms

"You're leaving with Gunner and me," his voice was sharp and clipped.

I looked up at him, trying so hard to calm my racing heart. My throat ached to prevent the tears from coming.

"No, Ratchet, I'm staying here. I don't belong with you, there's nothing you can do. Nothing you *should* do. Just let me be, I belong here."

"No, Sam! Fuck! Not doin' it."

I jerked myself out of his grasp. My hand shot out and I slapped him across the cheek. The loud music muted the sound of the slap, but we both felt it. His eyes became hard when he turned to face me again.

My voice came out loud and clear, "Just go away, Ratchet! I'm not a fucking charity case! Yeah, we fucked and all that. But I like to fuck! A lot! That's what I do. It was fun, but I'll make more money with the Hounds, better than working at some boring as fuck ass bookstore!"

The next thing I said was like a knife stab right to his heart.

"I know your mother didn't like that fuck-fest with your father's club. But she wasn't a club whore like me. Whores love to be passed around, that's just what whores like me do."

"I don't believe you, Sam. I know what you're doing and you're still leaving here with me. *Now.*"

"No. The little lamb is staying right here, Chaos King".

Vik appeared, the barrel of a gun pressed against the back of Ratchet's head.

Gunner's revolver was already out, aimed at the back of Vik's head, "He goes down? You go down."

Sid started to chuckle. Ratchet closed his eyes and raised his arms.

"Ok," when he opened his eyes, they were filled with so much pain, "I'm leaving Sam. If you run again, I'll be there to catch you."

He crushed me up against him and roughly claimed my lips, invading my mouth with his tongue.

He released me, defeat in his eyes. Vik lowered his gun.

Ratchet turned, walking away from me, "let's go, Brother."

Gunner's gun was shoved back into the front of his jeans. He followed, then they were gone.

CHAPTER TWENTY-SIX

RACHET

It started to rain as we left her there. My throttle wide open, Gunner close behind. The rain splattered our faces like stinging needles. The ache in the back of my throat was in high gear. My jaw clenched tight, twitching with the pressure. I failed to save my mother, now I failed to protect Sam. My father was right, I was weak, a pussy, just like he said. Images of my mother invaded my mind as I rode. Images of my father's club members. The sound of my mother's cries from behind the bedroom door. The memory of the sharp pain against the back of my skull.

My mind shifted to images of Sam laying on the asphalt beside the dumpsters. Visions of Sid and the Hounds hurting her; violating her.

A roar of defeat and anger came from my clenched jaw as I gripped the throttle, picking up more speed as we headed to the clubhouse.

The beam of my headlight spotted a wet grey thing on the gravel beside the road as I turned into the clubhouse lot. I parked, kick the stand down and walked back toward the damp grey thing. I knew it before I came upon it. But didn't want to believe it. Laying on his side, drenched entirely, half submerged in rainwater was the cat, Nomad. He must have been struck by a car as he walked across the road.

I went into the clubhouse and grabbed a shovel. I went back and picked up Nomad, carrying his already stiff body in the crook of my arm. I stopped by the tree line next to the asphalt lot laying him down and struck the wet ground with the shovel and started digging.

The heavy rain soaked through my hair, beard and clothes but I kept shoveling.

"Ratchet!" It was Gunner. "What are you doing, Brother?"

"Gotta bury him."

"Who's him?"

I nodded toward the soaked little grey body next to the hole I was digging. I stopped and leaned on the shovel.

"He came around a few times. Liked to rub up on my leg, so I fed him. He was a loner, just livin'. He took a liking to Sam the other morning too, we named him Nomad."

Gunner was silent, he just stood there with me, drenched as much as I was. I dropped the shovel and pressed my palms into my eye sockets until I saw little stars behind my lids.

"I'm a total fuckin' failure, Gunner and a dumb ass too. Thinkin' I could protect Sam, save her, I couldn't even save my mother," my voice cracked.

"Not your fault, Ratchet! You did the best for your mother. She did her best for you."

Gunner reached out and grabbed a fist full of my cut, pulling me to him.

"You better fuckin' cut the crap, Asshole. You're the best thing that ever happened to that girl, you helped her get out of her shell. You pushed her to go into that store and apply for that job. The club likes her. Tanya and her are becoming good friends. We just have to deal with all that giggling and chatting like all chicks do I guess. Your girl is brave, she's protecting you and Chaos. That's why she said those things."

"Well, it didn't do any good... The only way I can get her out is to go back. I will kill to get her out of there, bullets will fly next time and the damage will land me in prison or in the ground."

"And then where does that leave Sam? The

Chaos Kings? Your tribe? All that blowback will hit us."

"Well, I'm not left with many options, Brother. We're dealing with a diamond club. That's how things go down with that kind. You get your hands dirty - or bloody."

"Sid is a scum bag. He's weak. That's why he preys on Sam and anyone else he can. He likes to wag his dick and brag he's got the biggest in his pack of fuckin' dogs. And I'd bet he'd get a stiffy if he were offered a nice amount of cash to trade for Sam. I bet he would bite at that."

CHAPTER TWENTY-SEVEN

SAM

Ratchet and Gunner were gone. My mouth became dry as a desert. I had to fight back the tears again.

Slow clapping. Sid, Hammer, Rusty, Vik. *Clapping.*

"Didn't know you had it in you, Little Lamb," Sid praised as he approached me.

I walked to the other end of the bar where the dark-haired Hound sat finishing off his drink. I opened my parched mouth, "I never got your name…"

He slammed his small empty glass back on the bar, "It's Skully. Pour me another. Jack. Neat."

As I took his glass, Sid's father, Knuck walked through the front door; the President of the Hell Hounds MC. Sid had his father's tall, slender build, except his father had a few extra pounds of muscle due to all the weightlifting behind bars.

He walked up next to Skully, grinning at me.

"Prez…"

"Enjoy the pussy show, Skully. Then meet with Tweek when he gets his twitchin' ass here."

"Sure, Prez."

He turned back to me with the same piercing gaze as his son's.

"Well, well, well… Had to stop in to see it for myself. Good you came to your senses, girl. Sid needs to beat some sense into you, teach you a lesson. Don't try and pull that stupid bullshit again."

"Sorry, Knuck. Won't happen again."

"Now get me a shot of top-shelf whiskey with something cold back there."

Sid rose from his chair as his father approached him. Knuck backhanded him. Hard. The music was too loud, but I jumped when Sid's head snapped to his left. Knuck wore large gold and silver rings on all four fingers and they left the side of Sid's mouth bleeding. He reached up and wiped the blood onto his balled-up fist.

"Can't fuckin' keep the assets in working order,

son. You ain't President yet. Better fuckin' shape up or I'll rip that VP patch right off that fuckin' cut."

Knuck looked around. Skully, Rusty, Hammer.

"Who knows. One of these other dip-shits could do a better fuckin' job."

"Ain't gonna happen again, Knuck."

Knuck didn't even come back to the bar to get his shot and beer that I poured for him. He turned his back to Sid and left the club, leaving Sid standing there in silence. He realized everyone was looking at him, even the music had stopped and the girls in the cages stopped dancing.

"What the fuck is everyone lookin' at?" he barked. The DJ started the music again and the women continued dancing, pretending what they saw didn't happen.

Sid marched toward me. I back up against the shelves of liquor bottles, my adrenalin suddenly pumping through me, the fight or flight mode kicking in.

He lifted the bar latch and fisted a chunk of my hair and pulled me toward him.

"Come with me, Whore."

I followed him as he kept a tight grip on my hair and walked me down the hall to one of the private rooms before shoving me inside and shutting the door behind him. I turned to him. My instinct was to run at him or through him to get to the door.

But I stood there frozen, lifted my chin and looked right at him.

"Whatever you do to me right now, Sid you have already done before. So, what's it gonna be? A blowjob? Pass me around to your other Hounds? Sneak some drugs in for one of your other Hounds in jail? Pimp me out for a few days?"

His jaw was set. He came at me, grabbed both my arms, pushing me down to my knees. He started to unbuckle his belt and unzip his jeans.

"For starters, suck my dick you fucking slut!"

He reached and grabbed the back of my head and shoved himself into my mouth. He was barely hard.

He thrust into my mouth, his fist in my hair and dared me to pull back. I didn't. He was out of my mouth and pushed me back. I went back and landed on my right elbow.

"You can't even get my dick hard. You're just a waste of my time," he growled at me, his breathing fast.

He pulled me up to him and backhanded me just as hard as Knuck did to him. I landed back on the floor. Head spinning and ears ringing.

"Making me look like a faggot in front of my club? In front of the Knuck? Running off with that mother fuckin' Chaos?"

I pushed myself up and heard my own voice again.

"They call him, Ratchet. And he's a bigger man than you are, Sid. He doesn't have to beat women to get his dick hard. He doesn't have to prove himself to anyone. Least of all you."

"Bitch!"

Another backhand and my cheek landed on the floor this time. I didn't move. Sid stormed out the door and slammed it shut.

And that's when I could let the tears spring free, my body convulsed and I wailed. Thankful no one could hear me over the pounding music outside that door.

CHAPTER TWENTY-EIGHT

RACHET

Gunner made calls to Rocky, Spider, Magnet and Wez. Within a half hour, all club members were pulling in to the clubhouse. The steady rain turned into a cold mist.

They met Gunner and me at the bar inside. I already had two shots of tequila. Mud covered our boots and legs from digging the wet ground to bury Nomad.

I told my brothers what happened with Sam and that I was going to pay Sid to get her back; that I needed them *now* to keep watch and safeguard the clubhouse once this meet was done and I got her back there safe. No way to trust the Hell Hounds, I had to be one step ahead. They would take my money then kill me and Sam.

Early the next morning I pulled into the lot of the Hell Hounds clubhouse. It was a rundown, rusted out warehouse, in poor shape. A huge flat piece of sheet metal hung over the side door entrance, displaying the Hell Hounds center patch, a black dog with three heads, teeth bared and snarling. "Hell Hounds" was printed on top of the image, "Motorcycle Club" on the bottom.

I rode up toward the side entrance, pulled the clutch in then planted my feet. The Hound they called Skully leaned up against the rusted wall outside, smoking a cigarette. He was looking at me waiting. I let out the clutch and pulled up next to him.

"Skully?"

He flicked his smoke, "Yeah."

I dug out the folded piece of paper from my cut's side pocket and extended out it to him, "It's my number. Give it to Sid. Have a proposition for him."

He took the folded paper from me. I twisted the throttle, made a wide turn in the lot and left. Dangling a sweet amount of cash in front of Sid would have him frothing at the mouth. And he would be top dog in his club.

CHAPTER TWENTY-NINE

SID

I left Sam at the Steel Cage and rode back to the clubhouse. My blood was boiling over with anger. I needed to put a few bruises on soft female flesh. I walked into the clubhouse pulling one of the club whores off a bar stool and brought her into a bedroom that I played in many times with Sam and other whores.

This one was a redhead, really skinny but she had heavy tits that I pinched, slapped and pulled. She cried out at times. The sight of red blemishes appearing on her huge tits got me hard. She sucked me off and gagged as my hard thrusts pounded her mouth. I pulled out and shot my load all over her face. She wiped her face off with her own t-shirt. Pulling out a joint, she lit it and passed it to me. We both fell asleep on the creaky mattress.

I woke up to a wet warm mouth sucking me. I pulled her from me, my half hard cock slipping out of her mouth.

"Not in the mood now. Get the fuck out."

She left the bed and pulled on her cut off jean shorts. Her t-shirt was stained and crusted with my cum from the night before. She wiped her mouth, slipped her flip flops back on and left the room.

I sat up and lit a smoke. Three knocks on the door sounded.

"Fuck! What!"

Skully opened the door and stepped in.

"What's up, Skully."

"That Chaos just showed up here. Wanted you to have this."

I opened the folded piece of paper Skully handed to me, a 10-digit number to Ratchet's phone.

"Goddammit, Skully, that's it?"

"He said he had a proposition for you."

"He does, huh?... That fucker has got some balls coming here."

"I'm heading back over to the Cage. Meetin' up with Tweek."

CHAPTER THIRTY

RACHET

A number lit up on my phone. I knew it would be Sid. I answered on the second ring.

"Yeah."

"I'll give you one minute; then I gotta go back and shove my dick up that little whore's ass."

Silence on my end. I had to breathe through the rage. Calm the pounding in my head and ignore that ache in the back of my throat.

"I'll pay you. For her. Name the price."

"Whoa! You'd buy her? Why the fuck you

want that used up gash?"

"How much, Sid?"

Silence. Sid was nibbling on it. His dick was getting hard.

"Twenty-five."

"When?"

"Midnight. My clubhouse. Just you, Chaos."

"Deal."

I hung up. I already had twenty-five grand in cash. Wanted him to foam at the mouth over it. And hope that he wouldn't hurt Sam before I got her back. Leaving her there at the Steel Cage among the Hounds was the second time in my life that I would carry that heavy weight of guilt. It was tearing me up inside.

CHAPTER THIRTY-ONE

SAM

Sid kept me in the private room for the rest of the night and into the next morning. One of the dancers came in a few times to check on me. She gave me some ice in a plastic bag for my swollen lip. She showed a bit of empathy in her eyes. I was exhausted and slept on a black worn out leather couch with the blanket and pillow she gave me, the only acts of kindness I received that day.

I woke up touching the side of my cheek and wincing at the pain. It probably colored overnight to a shade of purple or blue.

Three knocks on the door.

"It's Skully. Brought you somethin' to eat." He walked in holding a brown paper bag and placed it on the couch next to me, "couple of donuts and a bottle of water."

I sat up on the couch and opened the bag.

"Thank you."

He didn't acknowledge me. His eyes moved to the floor searching for something. Then his eyes roamed over me.

"You wearing your jeans?"

"Yes, of course."

"Take them off under that blanket and give them to me."

Any of the Hounds could do what they wanted with me. I had to fend for myself.

"Not what you're thinkin'. I'm not here for that. Do you want Sid to come in and take 'em off you? Just give them to me."

He never touched or said anything nasty to me. I did as he said and wiggled myself out them and then handed them over.

He held them up examining them, "It shouldn't be *that* fuckin' complicated." He took out his pocket knife, switched it open and began tearing into the pant legs.

"What are you doing?"

"Making you a pair of ass-cheek cut-offs. Hold on. Never done this before."

He finished the one pant leg, cutting them off right below the back pocket and continued with the second one. When the last of the material fell to the floor, he held them up again.

"This should work. Put 'em back on. I'll get one of the girls to find you a top to wear."

My ripped-up jeans landed in my lap. Skully left me alone and I brought them under the blanket and wiggled myself back into them. I reached into the brown bag and devoured the donuts and finished the whole bottle of water.

Later the same girl from the night before came in and gave me a couple of tank tops to try on. I chose the leopard print and put on a pair of black wedge slip-on sandals. Along with my newly cut-off jeans, I looked the part of a club whore who worked at the strip club.

She also gave me a few things to freshen myself up with in the bathroom.

It was noon and I worked the bar. Three women started their first cage dances. Sid was sitting with Rusty and Skully at one of the small tables by the main stage. Sid looked smug, relaxed, taking another long drag off his smoke, talking to the two other Hounds at his table.

Three men appeared from the darkness of the front entrance into the disco colored light beams and black lights. They were huge, as wide as Ratchet, only they had very short haircuts and wore expensive looking designer suits. One had a fat cigar that he gripped between his teeth and nestled to the side of his mouth.

They took a seat at one of the semi-circle red velvet booths, their backs faced the back of the club. They watched the women dancing in the cages in the far corners.

I was staring at the big suited men and jumped when Vik suddenly appeared in front of me. His eyes roamed from my leopard tank top and cut-off jeans, lingering on my crotch and legs.

"You look good enough to eat, Little Lamb," he grumbled low, licking his bottom lip.

He nodded toward the three men at the booth but kept his eyes on my chest.

"See those three gentlemen over there? You go over and serve them what they want, arch your back some little lamb and shake that nice little ass when you walk over there."

"Tainted Love" by Marilyn Manson came on through the speakers. I grabbed a cocktail tray and walked over to them. They watched as I tried to do my best at a saunter, I stopped a few feet from the booth and smiled.

"Hi, gentlemen welcome to the Steel Cage, I'm Sam. What would you all like to drink?"

I didn't think they heard what I said as their eyes were fixed on my body. The one with the cigar took it out of his mouth and grinned.

"Do you dance too, Little Lamb?"

He had a Russian accent, thicker than Vik's.

* * *

"Ah. No. I just serve drinks," I stammered with a smile.

"Don't be shy, little one. Call me Demy and here are my close friends, Stan and Boris."

"Hello, Demy. I'm Sam."

I stood there frozen I just realized they didn't come here to have a drink or watch the dancers.

"You are very sweet, Sam. Now turn around for Demy."

My throat suddenly went dry and I fought back a cough, they wanted to appraise my body. I closed my eyes and turned around I felt warmth creep up from my chest to my scalp.

The beat of "Tainted Love" pounded in my ears as I stood there, my back turned to Demy and the other men, knowing their eyes roamed over my backside.

"Nice. Now you can get us a glass of your best Russian vodka."

I exhaled, realizing I held my breath and opened my eyes. I walked back to the bar to pour them their glasses of expensive vodka. My hand started to shake. The realization just hit me those men were Russians. They must know Vik. All three looked me over like I was on an auction block, they wanted to buy me. Sex trafficking.

Fear and panic punched my stomach. I poured

the vodka and walked back to them, placing the glasses on their table.

"Thank you, Sam," Demy raised his glass to me and took a drink.

Panic kicked in. I walked back, placed the tray on the bar and veered toward the front entrance to the club. The bass of the music reverberated throughout the place, red and blue beams of light rotating through the club, clouds of smoke billowing from tables enveloped me. I kept walking toward the front door. Only a few yards now. Keep walking, don't look back.

A hand suddenly grasped my upper arm and spun me around. "Where do you think you're goin' sheep?" It was Rusty. Grinning.

I froze, my eyes wide. I tasted bile rising in my throat from his touch. I dreaded him as much as Sid.

I tried to jerk my arm from his grasp.

"Let me go, Rusty! I'm not cool with this!"

He started to chuckle, he wrapped his arm around my waist and pulled me into his chest. He smelled of sweat, weed and liquor. I almost dry-heaved.

"Don't give a fuck what you think is cool or not, whore."

I struggled against him, grunting to get away, but that made Rusty chuckle even more.

"I like it when you try to fight back. Just gets my dick harder."

I suddenly felt the sting of his slap hard across

my cheek.

"Now shut the fuck up."

He released me but kept his grip on my arm, dragging me back into the club, away from the front door.

"Take her in the back, Rusty," Sid barked above the loud music. He sat down with the Russian men as I was trying to escape.

Rusty pushed me down the hall back into the same room I had slept in overnight. He stepped in after me I turned around to face him, ready for another slap or something worse.

"Now, keep your fuckin' mouth shut and stay in this room until Sid wants to fetch you." He turned, left and shut the door.

My heart was racing, bile rising again. I bent over and almost threw up the two donuts I'd eaten that morning. It was only a few dry heaves. I rose back up and screamed at the top of my lungs I was angry and frightened. Mad at myself for believing that Sid would take me back and everything would be like it was before. I was angry at myself for saying those horrible things to Ratchet in front of Sid and his disgusting Hounds.

CHAPTER THIRTY-TWO

SID

"Should've known she'd try to high tail it out. Good catch, Rusty," I sat with Demy and his two partners in the round booth, who witnessed the whole scene.

I turned from Rusty and back to Demy.

"She's just a little nervous but she's gonna clean up real nice. You won't regret it."

Demy blew out another cloud of cigar smoke, looking directly at me, uncomfortable silence for a few seconds.

"Have the little lamb ready by tomorrow morning at eight o'clock and you will have your payment. Do not disappoint us."

I reached my open palm out across the table to Demy.

"Thank you, Gentlemen."

Demy studied my palm for a moment. He shoved his cigar back in his mouth and reached out to shake.

"Now, let me and my men finish this vodka and be on our way."

* * *

"Pour us a shot of some good stuff back there, Brandy," I called out to the bartender the minute Demy and the two other Russian men left the club.

"Rusty, Skully, Tweek, Hammer, let's make a toast."

The drinks were poured and each of us grabbed a glass and took the shot. We slammed the glasses back on the bar.

"So, what's the plan, Sid? I thought we were gonna make bank and sell that whore off to Chaos."

Rusty asked too many questions. I had to hold himself back from reaching out and grabbing him by the throat again.

"What's up with the stupid fuckin' questions lately? We are, dumbass. We're gonna make bank with that Chaos motherfucker, but we're gonna make bank with my new business partner too. Demy will get the whore. That Chaos gets nothing but his own dick in his hand."

Rusty began to chuckle and Hammer followed along. I barked at Brandy the bartender again. "Pour us another fuckin' shot, Gash! Or do I gotta do your job for you?"

Brandy ran back from the end of the bar in her stilettos with the bottle of whiskey.

CHAPTER THIRTY-THREE

SAM

I knew there was always one of the Hounds outside the room that I was kept in all day. I was disgusted and sick to my stomach when I had to call out from inside to Rusty asking him if I could use the bathroom. He walked me to the women's restroom and watched me while I did the most private things, doing it in front of this sick perverted excuse for a man. I wouldn't look at him as I sat on the toilet, but I could feel his eyes on me and heard him chuckle low. By then I was past any feelings of embarrassment.

Once back in the room, Rusty wasn't done with me yet. He entered the room with me and shut the door behind him.

"Can't wait to see the look on that motherfucker's face when he realizes he don't get his whore back."

He stalked slowly toward me.

"Stay back, Rusty. Don't touch me you disgusting animal!" But he kept coming toward me, grinning.

"Oh, come on now whore... Just gonna shove my dick in your mouth one last time."

His strong hands grabbed my arms. I reached out and smacked him across the face and screamed. He just laughed.

"Fighting back just makes it more fun..."

Skully appeared at the door after three quick knocks.

Rusty didn't let me go but still turned toward him.

"What the fuck you want, Skully?"

"Sid sent me to watch the girl and wants you out there."

His eyes were on me.

"Fuck!" Rusty let me go and stomped toward the door, his face red with anger.

"If you fuck her, don't leave any marks. Those Russians won't like it."

Rusty walked out. Sully stood there staring at

me.

"You ok?"

"Yeah..."

He walked and shut the door closed. I sat on the couch and covered myself with the blanket I slept with the night before.

I didn't understand what Rusty meant? I thought they planned on selling me to the Russian men. Frenzied fear crept up on me suddenly. I only wanted to protect James and the Chaos Kings from the Hell Hounds. Once I came back to Sid and back to my Hell, I knew the quick taste of freedom and living my own life was never something I deserved anyway. Being cared for and treated like the most beautiful woman by Ratchet was something I would cherish forever. I crushed him when I said those horrible things. The look in his eyes made my heart ache more than any punch or slap I had ever felt upon my body.

I should have never trusted Sid to just keep me as *his* property and everything would be the same as it was before I had met James. He would never let that go, I made him look weak in front of the other Hounds and he was the VP.

I broke down and sobbed. That nightmare of drowning felt real at that moment I was alone. My life was stolen from me. My happiness was taken from me.

Thirty minutes later, those three knocks sounded from the door again. "It's Skully. I'm comin' in."

I was sitting on the couch; knees were drawn up to my chest, crying.

"We don't have much time. I'm getting you outta here. Let's go. *Now.*"

I looked up at him; he was standing half-way in, turning his head back to look down the hall. I didn't comprehend what he just said and didn't move. He looked back at me and I still didn't move.

"Now, Sam. Get your boots on and grab your lid. Let's go!"

I snapped out of it and sprang off the couch to put my boots on as fast as I could and grabbed my helmet. I followed him out of the room, down the hall toward the back door. I focused only on his back. I noticed he had a slight limp, but to some, it would seem it was just part of his gait. We headed out the back door. It was raining. I saw his bike.

He grabbed his helmet off the seat, strapping it on, "Is there somewhere close by that I can take you to?"

"My friend, Tanya. Her apartment," strapping mine on.

He got on the bike and started it. I jumped when it fired up, his pipes exploding with the rumbling sound. It could be heard from yards away.

"They left. No one can hear us in the club. Get on!"

He didn't have to tell me again. I hopped on behind him, he twisted the throttle and we took off. I yelled into his ear where Tanya lived. He did his best to take me down back roads. Riding above the speed limit and within ten minutes we were at Tanya's door at the second-floor apartment.

I knocked and knew Tanya could see me through the peephole. I heard her unlock the door, pull off the chain and she swung the door open.

Her eyes wide, she saw me standing next to Skully. She looked at him.

"Oh my god, Sam!"

She grabbed my arm and pulled me inside, then turned to Skully before he took a step. She moved toward him, only a foot away encroaching on his space. She craned her neck up to look at him. He was a foot taller than her.

"Who the fuck are you?"

Her protective instinct kicked in she didn't seem to care that he was a Hell Hound.

He looked down at her but didn't smile. It took him a few seconds to respond, "I'm Skully. That's who the fuck I am." He hooked his thumb into the side of his cut, overemphasizing to Tanya his patch. "I got Sam out and here to your place, Sweet Cheeks –"

"My name is *not* sweet cheeks. It's Tanya. And why did you do that?"

"It just wasn't right."

"It's ok, Tanya he should come inside too. They will be looking for him too when they find out I'm gone," I reassured her. He brought me to her safe I didn't think he would be any harm to us.

Tanya stepped back to let Skully into her apartment and shut the door. She grabbed my hand and walked me to her couch then wrapped me in her arms and sobbed.

"What happened, Sam? Are you ok? Does Ratchet know you're here?"

I clung to her tightly. To feel her holding me I felt safe again.

"No, Tanya I crushed him. I went back to Sid and the Hell Hounds on my own told Ratchet to go away…" I broke down and sobbed so hard my body shook.

She pulled me away from her embrace, "Sam; he's on his way to the Hound's clubhouse tonight. He made a deal with Sid to buy you for twenty-five thousand dollars."

"I thought Sid was selling me to those Russian men?"

"Yeah, he *is* selling you to the Russians."

We both looked at Skully, "And he's making the same deal with Ratchet too, but he isn't planning on giving you back to him. Kill two birds with one stone get rid of you and make bank."

That was Sid's way. He would have the money from both Ratchet and the Russians, be rid of me, proving himself to his club and his father.

Tanya grabbed her phone from the side table next the couch and scrolled through her contacts, "I'm calling Ratchet now. Talk to him, Sam."

CHAPTER THIRTY-FOUR

RACHET

All members of Chaos Kings, my tribe, were gathered at the clubhouse. I told them what was happening at midnight.

Rocky stood beside me. I looked out at all my brothers who were there for Sam and me. Gunner, Wez, Magnet, Spider.

"I owe all of you my life I don't trust Sid or any of them. I don't know if I'll walk out of his clubhouse with Sam, or alive for that matter. But I'm going to do what I fuckin' have to do. There will be blow-back and it will land here. At Chaos' door." I went silent. I didn't know what else to say.

"That's a fucked-up idea you goin' in alone. You know Sid's gonna have a few of his fuckers with him."

Rocky was hard to convince.

"I know, Prez. But I have to take my chances on this one." Then it hit me. I loved Sam. I would die for her. I would kill for her.

"I love this woman. Sam is real she's what I've needed all my life."

I said it and once I did, I knew it was real.

Some of my brothers nodded some even smirked or grinned back at me.

"Well, I can't fuckin' argue with that, Ratchet. You do what you gotta do and get Sam back here safe with Chaos."

Hollers, whoops and *fuck yeahs'* erupted from my brothers.

***

I left the clubhouse and got in my truck with the duffle bag that carried the twenty-five thousand in cash and headed out of the lot to Sid's clubhouse.

I pulled out of the area and my phone rang. I reached into the side pocket of my cut. Tanya's name lit up my screen.

"Tanya. You ok?"

"Ratchet? It's Sam…" It was her voice.

I slammed on the breaks as my heart skipped, "Sam! Where are you?"

Her voice came through the phone, shaky, faint.

"I'm ok, James. I'm at Tanya's apartment. Skul-"

I interrupted her. Didn't have time, "You and Tanya get to the clubhouse. *Now*, Sam. I'll meet you there in about 45 minutes."

"OK. We're going now ..." silence for a few seconds, "Ratchet... I'm so sorry for what I said- "

"No time for apologies, Rabbit just go now. That way I know you're safe."

My little rabbit did it again she got away. Escaped her Hell and came back to me. My heart settled back to a steady beat, but I gripped my steering wheel the whole way to the Hell Hounds clubhouse. My jaw clenched tight and ticked a few times. I had images of my mother, beaten and bruised. Then images of Sam beaten and bruised. I wanted to put my hands around Sid's throat and snap his neck. I kept that image in my head the rest of the way, picturing his sadistic face turn red and his eyes bulging, blood vessels popping in his eyeballs. Then those eyeballs saw nothing. Going blank after I heard the snap.

It was two minutes until midnight as I pulled into the Hounds clubhouse lot. I got out of my truck, grabbed the duffel bag and walked to the side door of the rusting building. No Hound was outside. They knew it was me.

I walked and took notice of the place. It was a rundown piece of shit. There were a few bar tables and chairs and bar stools, a pool table and a couch, but that's about it. Sid and Rusty both stood with arms folded and looked down at the duffle bag.

"Stop right there," Sid smirked at me, along with Rusty, "right on time Chaos."

I stopped about ten feet from both of them. "Twenty- five is in the bag. Where's Sam?"

Sid pulled the gun from his cut and aimed it at me. I'm guessing it was supposed to scare me. "She's not here. But she's still in one piece. Change of plans though. You leave the bag with us and scoot on back to your clubhouse. I'll deliver her to you there in two hours."

Rusty started up with a low fuckin' chuckle.

"Now, drop the bag and walk backward out the door."

I did just that, watching Sid and the gun still pointed at me.

"Now turn around. Leave Chaos."

As I walked out the door, shit came out of Rusty's mouth. Again.

"Don't worry, Asshole your whore is still in one piece. The Hounds are pullin' a nice long train on the bitch before you get her back."

I got in my truck and went *way* above the speed limit back to the clubhouse. I had to get there before the Hounds found out Sam was gone and I wouldn't be able to breathe until I saw her.

The sight of Tanya's car made me realize I was holding my breath when I exhaled, relief. Once out of my truck, I stomped to the entrance. My eyes scanned to see all my brothers, but not Sam. Not Tanya. My eyes turned back to one cut that stood out from all the rest. My mind suddenly registered and I recognized the cut – Hell Hound. Then the face – the dark-haired Hound who called himself Skully. The one I gave the message to.

Time stopped and now slow motion. All I saw was Hell Hound. All the pent-up rage exploded out of me. My legs moved. I roared while charging at him. I was quick enough. My left forearm smashed up into his throat. I pushed him up against the wall a few feet from where he was standing. He grabbed the front of my cut and slammed his eyes shut to the hard blow against him.

"If you fuckin' touched her, you're dead!" I growled, jaw clenched, eyes wide.

He opened his eyes. He had the same crazed look, "I didn't fuckin' touch her!" He shoved me back, even with my forearm planted against his neck.

"Stop, Ratchet!" Tanya's voice came from behind me. I felt her hand on my shoulder. "Skully got her out. He brought her to my place."

I dropped my forearm from his neck. He let go of my cut, breathing hard and grasping his throat, coughing, bending over. I turned around to Tanya and pulled her to me. She hugged me back tight.

"Tanya," I pulled her back to look at her. She had tears in her eyes, but she was smiling. "Where's, Sam?"

"She's in the bedroom. She's ok, Ratchet go to her."

I couldn't release Tanya fast enough. I ran down the hall to the bedroom. The bedroom we shared. When I opened the door, Sam was only two steps away then her body crashed into mine.

"My little rabbit... My brave, beautiful Samantha..."

She wrapped her arms around my shoulders. Her small body shook and she sobbed.

I pulled her from me to look at her. Lines of tears ran down her cheeks but she was smiling. She was smiling up at me. Her eyes. Her lips. No bruises.

"Are you ok? Did they hurt you? How did you get away?"

"I'm ok, Ratchet. Skully helped me. I don't know why, but he did. Sid is planning to sell me to some Russian men."

"I love you, Sam. I loved you the minute I saw you that first time. You're the real thing, Sam. The shit that's happened to you, things you've done before you came into my life, is the past. You're a survivor not a victim. You're free from your Hell now. You can live your life set your own destiny. But I need you in my life. Ride with me be my ol' lady."

More tears sprung from her eyes. The smile

left her face, her lips became a straight line. She shut her eyes tight and then opened them again, "I love you too, James. We were destined to find each other. Yes, I will be your ol' lady." She pressed herself back against me again and I held her.

Our lips smashed into each other. My hands roamed down her back. She was wearing only a t-shirt which she must have found in the room. Her body was so soft and warm.

"You're mine, Samantha and I'm giving you all of me."

I seized both her thighs and wrapped them around me. I invaded her mouth again and carried her to the bed. I laid her down and leaned over her. My big hands kneaded her softness.

Her lips pulled away from me. "Don't ever stop touching me, James," she breathed out against my ear.

"Get used to it, Sam. I'm never going to stop."

I couldn't wait another second. I had to be deep inside her. Claim her as mine. My hand snaked up under her t-shirt. I seized the side of her thong and tugged hard. It snapped and I ripped it away. She moaned and panted as I undid my jeans. The next second, I plunged my hard cock deep inside her warm soaked pussy. She cried out.

"Is this what you need, Little Rabbit?" I growled back in her ear, grinding my hips into her. I was rough, but I couldn't hold back.

"Yes, James! You give yourself to me oh so good!" She cried out.

I suddenly exploded deep inside her. I roared, feeling her soft wet walls wrap around my pulsing shaft.

The sound of pipes thundered through the walls of the room.

"That's them. Stay here."

I pulled out of her, pulling up my jeans.

"I'm sending Tanya back here with you."

I turned toward the door. She was a step behind me and grabbed my arm, "James, I'm scared!"

"It's ok. You're my ol' lady now. Nothing to ever be scared of again."

I pulled her back to me, leaned down and devoured her mouth. My tongue collided with hers and my rough hands cupped the cheeks of her soft ass. I pressed my hips forward and ground against her soft little body. She made that sexy low moan into my mouth. My empty cock jumped again.

I didn't want to, but I released her, "Now stay here with Tanya. I'll be back."

I headed out of the room and got to Tanya. Told her to go to the bedroom and stay with Sam. She didn't question me or hesitate. She heard the bikes too. By the time she shut the bedroom door, the Hounds were outside.

I walked outside, my tribe following close behind. Sid, Rusty and five other Hell Hounds, with their bikes still running. My Chaos brothers stood alongside each other.

"Bring that gimp mother-fucker out here

fuckin' *now!*" Sid barked out above the loud rumble of pipes.

Rocky took a few steps forward, "Not happenin'. You gonna gun us all down? Have every county cop here in 10 minutes? Cuz that's the only way you're getting past us to get to him. You're on Chaos territory. Get your pathetic one percenter asses off the property."

Sid's bike was still running, but he got off, letting go of the bars. The kickstand wasn't down and it crashed hard onto the asphalt as he came charging toward us. I collided with him. I grabbed him around the waist, picked him up off the ground and threw him down onto the asphalt, me landing on top of him. His breath was knocked out of him when his back hit the asphalt. I was up on my knees and braced myself above him. My fists came smashing down on his face. Left, right, then left again. Blood spurted from his mouth, his nose. His head was turning side to side against the hard blows my knuckles were giving him. I fisted the front of his cut and brought him up to my face.

"You think you're a man cause you beat on women?"

I let go and smashed my left fist into his face again. Again. And again.

"You're *dead!* Dead to Sam! Dead to Me! Dead to Chaos!" I emphasized with each pummel to his face. I couldn't stop. My left arm was held back suddenly and I stopped.

"I think you got your point across brother." It was Gunner. My brother.

I let go of Sid, his face bloodied, nose broken and got off him. He didn't move but then began to chuckle, his mouth full of blood.

I walked back with Gunner into the clubhouse. I looked down at my raw knuckles scraped and bleeding. I heard the pipes roar back up. The Hounds twisted their throttles again and then the sound faded away as they left.

CHAPTER THIRTY-FIVE

SAM

Ratchet took me home that night to his place. He carried me to his room and helped me take off the t-shirt and the jeans Skully tore into shorts. He shed his clothes too and we laid in his bed together. He wrapped his powerful arms around me and pressed his huge body against my back, keeping me safe as I slept. I didn't dream of drowning anymore. I dreamt of puppies and kittens.

I slowly woke up to slippery warm softness gliding up and down between my slit. My silky lips were spread open and the same slippery softness was discovered and he fondled my already swollen clit. It was sucked on softly, then flicked repeatedly. My hips began to move on their own, wiggling against that softness. My back arched and I opened my eyes. His sensual mouth tormented my clit with so much ecstasy I cried out.

"Oh, James. Your mouth. Your tongue. It feels so good."

I felt the vibration of his low moan on my pussy and I cried out again.

"You taste so sweet, Sam... I don't ever want to stop tasting you, pleasing you, fucking you and making love to you."

His finger slid into my wet hole as his tongue continued to fondle my clit making little circles over it faster and faster.

My hips rose up off the bed again to his mouth and delicious thrusting finger. My body suddenly exploded in orgasmic pleasure and I cried out, my walls clenching around his finger.

"Oh, James! I need you now. I need you deep inside me!"

"Yes, Sam. Gonna give you what you need right now."

His huge body moved up and over me. His engorged shaft filled me suddenly. He groaned, his hips pinned me beneath him. He gyrated and ground, his breathing shaky. He stretched me and buried himself deep. I cried out as he withdrew and thrust all the way back inside.

"You feel so goddam good, Sam. I can't hold back. I'm gonna fill you up... Right fuckin' now!"

I cried out as he exploded and filled me up deep inside. I felt him pulsate inside of me with his last drop he collapsed on me, both of us panting, with a sheen of sweat covering us.

"I love you, Samantha," he whispered next to my ear a few moments later.

"I love you, James."

James took me to the bookstore a few days later. Kat was in tears and sobbing as she hugged me tightly.

"I'm so sorry, Sam! I should have done something!"

I pulled out of her tight hug, "You *did* do something, Kat. You helped save me. You called Ratchet. James."

She smiled at me and pulled me in again for another tight hug and I cried with her.

I still had my job, so all was good with that. James suggested and I told Kat she was invited to come over to our place sometime for dinner and to join us at the Chaos clubhouse the next time we have a party. I would introduce her to some caveman bikers. They looked intimidating and scary on the outside but can be tame teddy bears around the females. She blushed and told me she would take me up on the offer soon.

James got word from among other clubs and

bikers in the county that Sid wouldn't be able to walk again. Knuck found out about the deal he made to sell me to the Russians, plus extorting the twenty-five thousand from James and the broken nose and busted teeth that James gave him.

"That worthless piece of shit VP of a one percenter club got a little too greedy. Knuck was pissed beyond belief. But he wasn't gonna go toe to toe with the Russians. So, he let them have Sid."

James shook his head telling me this as we sat at the table eating the eggs, sausage and toast he made for breakfast.

"When the Russians discovered you weren't there for delivery; they beat the shit out of Sid, to the point where he almost died. Unfortunately, he lived, but he'll be shacked up at Stayford Hospital in a body cast."

Rusty and the other Hounds were searching for Skully. James still didn't like him and wouldn't have cared if Chaos handed him back over but he did help get me out. He left the clubhouse once the sound of the Hounds' pipes could no longer be heard. He left on his bike and we hadn't heard anything of him since. He was on the run I figured he might have split town.

* * *

I played with my scrambled eggs; my mind consumed with images of Sid. Bruised, beaten, bones were broken and his body encased in a plaster cast in a hospital bed. Those were images I could save and pull up for those times when we got swallowed up and rode that anxiety roller coaster.

James reached and brought my chin up with his forefinger and tapped it lightly to bring my eyes up to his. The side of his mouth lifted into a crooked smile, "Nice images, huh Little Rabbit?"

His eyes were the color of brandy. Looking at me made my heart beat faster.

"Yes, but I'd much rather have images of my ol' man fucking me so good he makes me walk funny afterward."

His eyebrows lifted in surprise. Yes, I said that. He reached over, grabbed the seat of my chair and dragged me over to him.

"Come here, my little rabbit. We're done with breakfast. Now it's time to make you walk funny as you requested. For the rest of the day…"

* * *

I reached up to rub my nose when something soft tickled it. I felt it again. I scrunched my nose. I was in between that fogginess of sleep and wakefulness. A soft, high-pitched purr came to my sense of hearing. I opened my eyes to see a pair of eyes, cat eyes looking at me. My blurry vision focused on a little white kitten. Its tiny paw touched my nose and mewed. I sat up suddenly James was standing beside the bed with a half smirk on his face.

"I never had any pets growin' up as a kid. I

liked Nomad. He was a loner, but he liked to rub up on me and you too. I went to the local shelter this morning. They had a bunch of these little cats in a cardboard box so, I picked this one."

I picked up the tiny little soft furry thing. It mewed at me and batted and pawed at strands of my long dark hair.

"They're called kittens, James."

I had an adorable image of my big lumbering ol' man picking up kittens out of the box.

"I got it some things like food and toys and a litter box. That's what the clerk at the pet shop told me I needed and we need to take it to a vet for a check-up and shots. Or something like that."

I raised the kitten up to check the sex.

"And this kitten is a female."

I brought her back down to cradle her in my arms. Her fur was so soft and white and she was the cutest thing I had ever seen.

"So, what do you want to call her?"

James tilted his head, watching me cuddle her.

"Gypsy. Can we call her Gypsy?"

James' mouth lifted into a full-blown grin.

"Yeah, Sam. Let's call her Gypsy."

THE END

ACKNOWLEDGMENTS

To my Mother and Sisters, Rie, Debbie and Darice – Thank you for being so supportive and loving me no matter what.

To Norman – Thank you for teaching me the biker lingo and supporting me on my journey as a romance writer. Because of you, I know what Shovelheads, Panheads, Knuckleheads and Flatheads are.

To Jeanette George – Thank you for being my pep-rally when I started writing this book. You helped me with an awesome book blurb! Thank you for listening to me vent over the years. Even though living in separate states, you are one of the true friends I've ever had. Never forget our fangirl love for Anne Rice and our trip to New Orleans together.

To Tonyna at Primrose Passage – Thank you for all your help and expertise in the indie author world. You ROCK!

To Jeanna Bini – Thank you for all your expertise as my critique partner. When I started writing, I hit a wall and didn't know where I was going with the story. And now my skills as a writer are getting better because of you.

Shari Slade – Thank you for your awesome-sauce Book Babe Boot Camp! I learned so much about marketing and branding. You are an inspiration to all the book babe indie authors out there like me.

ABOUT THE AUTHOR

Linny grew up in Northern Virginia, right outside Washington DC and has a professional career in sales operations for over 20 years. She's also spent 13 years riding with her husband on the back of a Harley! Linny loves the feeling of freedom, wildness and rebellion that comes with it. The biker community can be tribal and primal at times.

Linny has also been a huge book worm since she was a young teen. She reads different genres of books, but the one Linny loves the most is Romance! She self-published her debut novel, "Salvation in Chaos" in January of 2018. Her stories are about scruffy, sexy alpha bikers who belong to a tribe, their club and the women they fall in love with. They live in a world full of chaos, not unlike reality. But within that chaotic world, they live their lives the best way they can and discover true love.

SOCIAL MEDIA

Facebook page:
https://www.facebook.com/Linnylawlessromance
Chaos Coven Clubhouse:
https://www.facebook.com/groups/1481551685255
429
Website:
https://linnylawless.com
Instagram:
https://www.instagram.com/linnylawless
Goodreads:
https://www.goodreads.com/user/show/73729078-
linny-lawless
BookBub:
https://www.bookbub.com/authors/linny-lawless

OTHER BOOKS BY LINNY LAWLWSS

"Salvation in CHAOS"
"Deep in CHAOS"
"Coveted by CHAOS"
"Claimed in CHAOS"
"Summer Heat" Anthology

<u>Coming Soon:</u>
"Conquered by CHAOS"
"PUSHED"

52534247R00114

Made in the USA
Columbia, SC
10 March 2019